Dead Silence

A Village Library Mystery, Volume 13

Elizabeth Spann Craig

Published by Elizabeth Spann Craig, 2025.

To Rebecca Wahr for her generous help with the concept. Thanks!

Chapter One

"Fitz, could you let me look at that magazine you're lying on?" Grayson gave my orange and white cat a pleading look. The periodical in question was a wedding magazine, and I'd just mentioned an article on groomsmen's gifts that I thought Grayson might find useful.

Fitz blinked at my fiancé, rolling over onto his back instead of removing himself from the magazine altogether.

"He wants you to pay a toll," I said with a laugh. "You're going to have to rub his tummy."

Grayson reached out to love on Fitz. "I know Fitz is an incredible cat who really redefines what it is to be a feline. But I'm still a little timid when it comes to rubbing any cat's belly."

Fitz, however, was clearly loving it, smiling a feline smile with his eyes halfway closed. And, after a minute or two, he got off the magazine and into my lap.

Grayson and I were at my cottage, poring over wedding magazines and trying to plan our big day. We'd decided that it was a big *day*, not a big *event*. We didn't want anything too swanky, too glitzy. The feel we were going for was warm, cozy, simple, and genuine. A happy day, surrounded by friends.

But still, wedding magazines were a must. It was fun to look at all the ideas, even if we discarded most of them outright. The wedding gowns ranged from classically basic to truly off-the-wall. I worked at the library, after all. It was easy to check out a bunch of older periodicals to look at in the comfort of my home.

"I wonder if having me over here all the time will be a tough change for Fitz," said Grayson, flipping through the magazine to find the groomsman article. "After all, he's used to having you all to himself, without having to share."

I shook my head. "I don't think jealousy is in Fitz's chemical makeup. He's sort of a 'the more, the merrier' type of cat. An extrovert."

Perhaps to prove the point, Fitz climbed into Grayson's lap, looked soulfully into his eyes, then snuggled up. We both laughed, and Grayson gently rubbed the cat.

Grayson had gamely come over to look at the magazines, but I could tell he was totally wiped out from his day covering news for our small town. Like Fitz, Grayson was also an extrovert. This meant that days mixing with the good residents of Whitby was ordinarily something that energized him. But today seemed the complete opposite.

"Everything go okay today? I know you were covering the last-minute preparations for tomorrow." It was July 3, and the next day was Whitby's annual (and beloved) Independence Day celebration. There was a parade, a play, and lots of red, white, and blue.

Grayson gave me a wry look. "Is it that obvious? Sorry. I thought I was more scintillating company than I probably am."

"You're always scintillating. What happened at work?"

Fitz looked up at Grayson with an inquiring look. Grayson tickled him under his chin, making Fitz give a delighted purr. "Oh, it was just hectic. The Whitby Playhouse volunteers were everywhere, since they always help with setup and takedown for big town events. Pete Brennan was frantically reworking the parade route, for reasons unknown. Then there's the evening performance of *The Spirit of '76*. You know, the patriotic play they're doing after the parade. Rebecca Thorne was practicing her Martha Washington walk and kept saying she wasn't getting it right, while David Hollister, who's directing the whole production, was trying to keep everyone calm and on schedule."

"How would Rebecca even know what Martha Washington's walk was like?"

"Exactly!" said Grayson, beaming at me. "That's exactly what I thought. Then Carol Winters was documenting everyone's mistakes as a sort of self-appointed director, which wasn't helping David's stress levels at all."

"Maybe Carol was the person critiquing Rebecca's unimpressive Martha Washington walk," I offered.

"Entirely possible." Grayson sighed. "But enough of that. I managed to take the day's events and somehow transform them into what will hopefully read as a compelling article for tomorrow's paper. Now I'm moving on to more interesting things like spending time with you."

He reached out to give me a hug, being careful not to disturb Fitz. Then he laid down the wedding magazine. Grayson seemed as if he had something on his mind, but wasn't sure how to broach it. I just waited, figuring that prompting him to spit it out would backfire.

Finally, he said cautiously, "I was thinking about where we'll live after the wedding."

It had been weighing on both our minds lately. After all, our wedding wasn't some distant dream. We were planning something intimate and manageable, hoping to marry in the next few months. But we'd made no progress on the question of where we'd actually live afterward.

I was settled in my great-aunt's cottage, while Grayson still lived in his larger place in the neighborhood. There was a big part of me that dreaded the thought of leaving this cottage, even though I knew it wasn't practical. This was where I'd grown up, where every corner held a memory I treasured. But the reality was unavoidable. We simply wouldn't have enough space once we combined our lives.

"Did you come up with any ideas?" I asked.

Grayson abandoned his caution, eagerly asking, "What if we live here?"

"Would we have the room?" I knew the answer was no, but I didn't want to be the one to say it.

"We could expand it," he continued enthusiastically. "I know how much you love this place—its character, its garden. I hope you don't mind, but I took the liberty of asking an architect friend to draw up some preliminary sketches." He looked anxiously at me. "Was I out of line? You probably want to preserve the cottage, not change it."

I shook my head, smiling at him. "I want to be here if it's practical. If we can make that happen, that would be amazing."

Grayson looked relieved. He reached for his backpack and pulled out some papers, spreading them out so I could see. "Like

I said, this is totally preliminary—just to give us a starting out place to figure out what you might want or not want. Obviously, it would mean losing a little space in the backyard, though."

I looked through the drawings. "I love that it looks like it has the same footprint on the front of the house, though. Your friend tried to keep the character of the place intact."

"Well, that's what I asked for. Again, I didn't want to step out of line. I was just excited about the possibility of staying here and wanted to get an idea what that might look like. We can go in any direction you want to. Or scrap the idea altogether." Grayson looked at me a bit anxiously.

"No, I really like this idea. And the thought of going in any direction we want to." I glanced over at Fitz, who was looking fetchingly at Grayson to get him to keep petting him. Grayson quickly obliged. "Fitz would like a sunroom, wouldn't you, Fitz?"

Fitz's expression said that he absolutely would.

Grayson gave me a grin. "We could also use another small bedroom, thinking toward the future. And I was thinking again about the size of our combined book collections. Maybe we need a library, too."

"Well, I can tell you that an open floor plan definitely wouldn't work. We'll need lots of wall space for bookcases." Then I frowned. "Why do I have the feeling Zelda will have a fit over us building an addition? You know she's on the architectural review board for the homeowners association."

Grayson said, "Oh, you know Zelda loves you. She'll sign off on anything you want to do to your cottage."

I arched my brows. "Are we talking about the same Zelda? I'm talking about the one that lives in our neighborhood, has henna-red hair, and is on the HOA board."

"I'm sure you won't have any trouble at all. That *we* won't have any trouble at all."

The late hour, or late relatively speaking, was finally catching up with me. I covered my mouth with my hand to conceal a tremendous yawn. "Sorry," I said. "It's not the company."

Grayson glanced at his watch. "Oops. I didn't mean to keep you up this late. Or myself up this late, actually. We both have an early start tomorrow morning."

I nodded. "I think it was awesome they chose someone from the library to be the parade grand marshal. But Wilson would have made a better pick."

"Are we talking about the same Wilson?" asked Grayson in a teasing voice, copying me from earlier. "I mean, I love the guy, don't get me wrong. But he can be a little aloof."

"I don't know if I'd call him aloof. He's very formal, though."

"And stiff," added Grayson.

"That could just be age," I demurred.

"Let's just say you're the far better candidate for smiling and waving from a float in a July Fourth parade," said Grayson.

I grinned at him. "Well, thank you. Fingers crossed it all goes well. I kept checking the weather today, hoping there weren't going to be any errant storms."

"From what I saw, it should be great tomorrow." Grayson extricated himself from Fitz with some difficulty, then leaned over to plant a quick kiss on my lips. "I'll see you on Main Street tomorrow morning. What time are they having you come in?"

"Eight o'clock."

Grayson nodded. "I'll already be there by that time. See you then."

When I arrived downtown the next morning, there were already families lining the streets to get good spots for the parade. I could see David Hollister at the gazebo doing last-minute work on the bunting and banner anchors. I supposed they'd run out of time the night before. There were lots of red, white, and blue, and American flags. I walked down to the start of the parade route, where floats were parked at the ready. The air buzzed with excitement and the smell of kettle corn from the nearby food trucks. I could hear the high school marching band warming up in the distance, running through snippets of 'Stars and Stripes Forever,' while younger children squealed with delight as they spotted the elaborate floats.

After I signed in, I was the surprised recipient of a sash and a bouquet from the parade committee. Librarians aren't exactly used to such treatment, and the committee member who gave them to me laughed at my startled expression. "This is standard procedure," she assured me.

I was happy to represent the library. Wilson, the library director and my boss, was pleased as punch that I was the grand marshal. So smile and wave I would, with flowers and sash and whatever else was required.

I broke into a grin when I spotted Luna, my library coworker, walking up to me. Luna was something of a spectacle even on a regular day with her colorful, wild outfit combinations, piercings, tattoos, and hair color of the day. But she'd really outdone herself for the Fourth of July. She wore a skirt with white stars appliqued on it, a blue peasant blouse with bell sleeves, red, white, and blue striped tights, and comfortable sandals with ribbons in patriotic colors.

Before I could even greet her, Luna thrust her phone at me. "I haven't even had the chance at work to show you the pictures from the trip Jeremy and I took."

"Yeah, work's been nuts lately. At least we get a break today," I said, peering at some blurry images on Luna's phone and trying to make sense of what I was seeing. Luna wasn't the best at photography, and I wasn't sure if I was looking at a picture of a landscape or a human being.

"Do we even have a break? Maybe I do, but you're here representing the Whitby Library." Luna said. She looked at something behind me and her face brightened. "Oh, and there's Wilson!"

I wasn't surprised Wilson would show up at the parade. He was, after all, delighted about the library's recognition represented by my being the parade grand marshal. I asked, "How are things going with Wilson and your mom?" The two had been dating for some time. To me, they were proof that opposites can attract. Wilson is always rather staid and crusty. Mona is bubbly and warm. Together, however unlikely, they appear to make a great team.

"Oh, I guess they're going fine. It's a little weird to see so much of Wilson after hours. But I'm glad my mom has fun stuff to do with someone. Someone besides me, at least," said Luna. She quickly cut herself off as Wilson drew up alongside us. "How are things going, Wilson? Big day for the library, isn't it?"

"It certainly is," said Wilson a bit vaguely as he peered over to look at the float I was about to ride on. The theme was "Reading Through History," and it was basically a flatbed trailer decorated as a vintage reading room, complete with a faux fireplace, oversized books, and period furniture. There was a raised armchair that I gathered was to be my perch during the parade.

Apparently, the float garnered Wilson's approval. He gave a satisfied bob of his head. "Marvelous," he said. "I wasn't at all sure how this was going to work. But seeing it finished, it did all come together." His voice was relieved, as if he'd been quite sure it wouldn't have.

A moment later, Timothy joined us. He was a teenage library film club regular, and one of our most valuable library volunteers. Not only did he help the public with our scheduled tech days, he was now assisting with the sound system on the float. "Hey there," he said in his typical upbeat way. "Is it okay if I get the PA system set up? I'll need to do a sound check before the parade starts."

Wilson nodded. I tilted my head to one side. "PA system? I'm not supposed to make a speech, am I? No one mentioned that, and I haven't prepared anything."

Timothy shook his head. "Nothing like that. We've just got recorded patriotic music running on a loop."

Wilson murmured for us to excuse him, and he busied himself closer to the float. Luna said, "Are you enjoying your break from school this summer?"

Timothy grinned. "Well, I'm not sure it's much of a break. You know I'm homeschooled. My mom has me volunteering all summer to build up my college applications."

Luna said, "And the library is totally grateful for it! You're like our tech wunderkind." She turned to me. "Is there anything Timothy doesn't know how to do?"

"If there is something, I haven't come across it yet," I admitted. I saw Owen hanging back in the background a little. He was years younger than Timothy, had gone through some rough times, and looked up to Timothy as not just a friend but a mentor. "How are things going, Owen?"

He brightened, giving me a contented smile. "Everything's great. Timothy is showing me the ropes for the sound system."

"That's good. You're going to be a prodigy yourself, at this rate," I said. Then I turned back to Timothy. "You're up next for film club, right?" I hosted film club at the library, where the members took turns selecting and discussing interesting movies. Timothy was an avid movie buff.

"I thought I'd do an oldie but goodie. I'll make the big reveal of the movie at film club."

Luna said, "I might have to join up with you guys during film club, at least for a few minutes. Although it depends on whether the children's section is crazy or not. And it's fairly crazy ninety percent of the time."

I noticed Owen taking in our conversation with interest. "Owen, would you like to come to film club, too? It's a black-and-white movie, but it's a wonderful movie, if you don't mind old films."

I could tell he wanted to come from the wistful look on his face. But I also knew his mom was currently working two jobs to make ends meet. He was staying at his house, since school was out for the summer, but was out fairly often thanks to Timothy's generosity. Owen hesitated. "I'd like to, but I don't have a ride."

Timothy grinned at him. "No worries. I'll come by and pick you up. It's too good to miss." He glanced at a large watch on his thin wrist. "We'd better get this sound system checked. We're getting too close to time. We've got some banners to put up, too." The two boys hurried off, clambering up onto the library float.

I turned to Luna. "Have you seen Grayson around anywhere?"

"Oh yeah. He's been running all over the place. Taking lots of pictures, too. I thought he had a photographer for stuff like that."

I said, "He does, but it's July Fourth, so there are folks out on vacation. Small-town newspaper, you know. Luckily, Grayson can do everything."

One of the parade organizers strode up then to give me some last-minute instructions. As a grand marshal, my role was basically fairly symbolic and ceremonial. My job was waving and smiling and hopefully drawing attention to the library. I'd been stunned when they'd offered the role to me. The library board nominated me, the organizers said, because of my personal service record. To me, it was just part of my usual job to help patrons with research, job applications, technology, and other issues. They apparently also liked that I'd spent most of my life in Whitby. I'd been surprised and a little uncomfortable at the attention, but Grayson and Luna had persuaded me to accept it.

Forty-five minutes later, the parade was off and running. Or perhaps up and walking is a better way to put it since we moved at a very sedate pace. The parade kicked off with Burton, our police chief, in the lead police car, his window down as he waved to the crowd, giving a cheerful whir of his siren that made the children along the route cheer. I smiled and waved enthusiastically as folks along the parade route waved small flags while the floats went by. I passed Wilson, who now had Mona by his side in the crowd. He gave an approving nod at me.

The sound system was indeed working well as the strains of 'It's a Grand Old Flag' came through our float's speaker. Fortunately, the high school marching band was some distance behind me as their sound was far stronger than our speaker system.

I glanced up when we passed the town's gazebo, now strung with bunting in red, white, and blue. Then I frowned, peering closer. Although it was in the distance, there seemed to be someone lying down on the cement. There were benches in the gazebo, but the form I was seeing wasn't on them, but on the floor. Something dark lay on the ground nearby. It looked like a tool of some kind.

I'd already passed Wilson and Mona, so I glanced around to see if I could spot anyone else who could check on the person in the gazebo. It was hot out, of course, being July. I hoped they'd just passed out from the heat. I looked around for Burton, our police chief and my friend, but I saw another officer in blue instead. I managed to get his attention as we were approaching his spot in the crowd.

He spotted me immediately and started walking next to my float. "The gazebo," I said. "It looks like somebody might need help. They're lying on the cement floor."

The cop nodded curtly and swiftly turned to make his way up to the structure. I wanted to watch to see what was happening, but I had completely different responsibilities at the moment, none of which entailed investigating what was probably somebody's health problem. I resisted the urge to turn and watch the officer's progress.

A couple of blocks later, I saw Grayson, camera around his neck. He blew me a kiss, and I smiled back at him. I felt myself relax a little. Whatever happened to the person in the gazebo was being handled by the police.

Minutes later, however, I spotted Burton, now out of his cruiser and on his radio, looking grim before heading up toward the gazebo.

Chapter Two

The rest of the parade was a blur for me. I was smiling and waving as instructed but have no doubt I probably looked distracted and robotic. As soon as I'd reached the end of the parade route, I hopped off to get an update.

I was stopped along the way by a few patrons chatting about the library float and my role as marshal. It was probably fifteen minutes later that I finally made it up to the gazebo.

By this point, I saw a couple of unmarked vehicles and some men and women in civilian clothes who appeared to be investigating. It looked like Burton had called in the state police, or SBI.

Grayson was already up near the gazebo, watching and waiting his turn to speak with Burton. He turned to look at me. "Hey there."

"Have you heard anything about what's happened?" I tried to look into the gazebo, but there was crime scene tape and too many people to get any sense of what had occurred.

Grayson nodded grimly, looking back over at the structure. "I'm afraid so. It's David Hollister. It looks like he's been murdered."

"David? Oh no." I didn't really know David well, but I'd met him a couple of times. "I couldn't tell who it was from the float. I saw him up at the gazebo earlier today, working on getting the decorations set up."

Grayson turned back around. "You're the one who spotted him?"

I nodded. "As the float was passing the gazebo. I spotted a figure lying down on the floor there. I got the attention of a cop, and he walked up to check it out. I was hoping it was just someone with a medical emergency. Something related to the heat maybe." I paused. "You're thinking it's murder because of all the police presence? Or did you see something up there?"

"It looked like David was struck with something heavy. I could see there was a rubber mallet nearby. It was one of the big ones the theater uses for building sets," said Grayson in a low voice. Bystanders were starting to appear.

"It's hard to believe somebody would choose such a public place to murder somebody. And on a major holiday, too. Whoever did this has got to have a screw loose."

"Or maybe was really desperate?" asked Grayson.

I said, "You know David better than I do. Can you think of anybody who'd be desperate enough to kill him under these circumstances?"

Grayson considered the question. "The only person who comes to mind right now is Rebecca. She's his ex-fiancée."

"Their relationship didn't end well?"

Grayson gave a small shrug. "It was something David didn't want to really talk about. But I could tell there was tension there even before the two of them broke up. Going from being engaged to breaking up is a huge step."

We looked at each other, and I thought about our own relationship. I couldn't imagine scrapping our wedding plans to live totally separate lives. I wondered what could have happened between David and Rebecca for them to have made that decision.

I spotted Burton walking up to us, looking solemn. He motioned for us to follow him a bit out of the way, farther from the collecting bystanders. "Remember, we're off-the-record right now, Grayson," he said right off the bat.

"Of course," said Grayson quickly.

Burton turned to me. "You've had quite a morning. My deputy told me you'd flagged him down after you saw the body in the gazebo."

"I was up on a perch, so I had a better view. And, of course, everyone's attention was pointed toward the parade, not away from it."

Burton nodded. "You were on the first float, behind me, weren't you?"

"That's right."

Burton took out a small notebook and a stub of a pencil to jot that down. "That helps us establish a timeline. What exactly did you see from the float? Can you describe the position of the person?"

I said slowly, "I saw a figure lying on the gazebo floor, not on the benches. That stood out to me right away. The body seemed to be on its back, but in an awkward position. I remember wondering if maybe somebody had a health issue. Like heat stroke or something. But thinking back on it now, it almost looked more like someone would appear after a fall." I paused. "I understand it's David Hollister?"

"It is," said Burton. "But I'll need both of you to keep quiet about the details until we have the chance to notify the family."

Grayson and I both quickly agreed. Burton continued, "Did you see anybody hanging out in the immediate area of the gazebo, Ann? Anyone behaving suspiciously?"

I shook my head regretfully. "No. I kind of zeroed in on him. But from what I remember, there was no one in the area. After all, anybody out here was here for the parade. They were all lining the street."

Burton made a couple more notes on his notepad. "Okay. Thanks for your quick action this morning. I'd have hated if one of the kids at the parade had been the one to come across him."

Grayson had confirmed to me that there was a rubber mallet on the scene, but I wanted to see what Burton might say about it. "I also saw something that looked like a tool on the ground near David."

Burton said, "A mallet. David was apparently using it to drive in stakes for the decorations. The mallet had 'Property of Whitby Playhouse' written on it in a black marker. David, of course, was one of the theater volunteers. Again, all this is information you'll need to keep to yourselves."

We nodded. Then, before Burton left, Grayson gingerly said, "Burton, I understand this is off-the-record. But as editor, I need to know what I *can* report and be responsible about it. Can you give me the basics for public information? What's helpful for the community to know versus what might compromise your investigation?"

Burton bobbed his head in a nod. "You can give confirmation that a body was discovered during the July Fourth festivities. Giving the location is okay, as well as that the SBI has been called to assist. No mention of murder: just use standard language that the investigation is ongoing. And, if anyone saw anything, ask them to contact the police."

Burton turned to me. "Ann, you're a witness, so I can't have you quoted about what you saw right now."

Grayson asked, "Can I mention that a parade participant alerted the police, without naming Ann?"

Burton considered this. "How about 'a parade observer noticed someone in distress and alerted authorities.'"

One of the state police called out to him, and Burton headed swiftly away.

Grayson reached out to squeeze my hand. "I hate to say it, but I need to run, too. I've got to find out if the rest of the festivities are going on or if they're canceled. Our social media will need to be updated. Are you okay?"

"I am. Although I feel awful for David." I frowned. "Was he close to Jeremy? I remember they worked together." Jeremy was a friend Grayson met when he'd moved to Whitby. He was now dating Luna.

Grayson said, "They were definitely work friends. I don't know how close they were outside of the office." He frowned. "Obviously, I can't tell him anything about what happened. Burton has to notify David's family."

I frowned, thinking about it. "His sister is Angela, right?"

"That's right."

As Grayson left to return to work, I walked back to the town hall, which was the staging area for the parade participants. I was just going to grab my purse and keys and head out, but slowed down when I heard a couple of people talking about what had happened. Apparently, both of them were in the play that was supposed to go on that night.

A man was saying, "I just don't know how they expect us to perform tonight after all this."

A woman answered him. "You don't know who it was?"

"No, but it doesn't matter who it was. All I know is that I heard there was some kind of death at the parade. It feels wrong for us to have the play after something like that. You know? It's a tragedy."

The woman said, "Well, they always say that the show must go on, right? We've put a lot of time and effort, not to mention the cost of costumes and the sets, into making this happen."

Then another woman came in. I recognized her as Carol Wilson. She was a retired drama teacher; in fact, I'd been in her class when I was in high school. I remembered she was still involved in the community theater. She was in her mid-sixties and, as usual, was in a perfectly coordinated outfit with costume jewelry and sensible shoes. She'd obviously caught the tail end of the conversation.

"We've got more problems than just feeling insensitive about going ahead with the play," said Carol briskly. "That was David who died."

The other two showed shock at the news. One of them said, "No way. I can't believe it."

"It's true," said Carol grimly. "So this isn't just a tragedy because someone from the community died. It's someone who was directly involved with our production. Someone we all knew."

"Not just directly involved," said the man, sounding worried. "The *director*. How are we supposed to go on without the guy in charge of everything?"

Carol said, "I think we probably have to. Like Lynn was saying, we've put a lot of time, effort, and money into the production. People have bought tickets. Besides that, I think David would have wanted us to go ahead with the show."

The man said, "Yeah, but is that decision even up to us? The town might want to call off the plans for the rest of the day. I heard somebody else saying there was going to be a meeting to see whether it was appropriate to continue the festivities or not."

"Then we'll go to the meeting and tell them what we think. What time is that supposed to be?" asked Carol.

"Two o'clock," answered the man.

"Here at town hall?"

He nodded.

"Let's show up and persuade them that we should move ahead with *The Spirit of '76*. We can offer to have a moment of silence at the start and then talk about David's contribution to the show at the end," said Carol.

Both the man and the woman murmured agreement. Then the woman said, "Was this just a medical emergency, Carol? A heart attack or something?"

Carol's voice was brisk again. "No, nothing natural. It was murder."

Both the others exclaimed again. Then the woman said slowly, "David seemed really wound up about something lately. Not just the play."

Carol said, "I agree. I thought at first it was just the performance, but he was acting like his mind was elsewhere the last week or so."

More people came into the staging area to pick up their things, and their conversation broke off. I walked out, purse and keys in hand. What had David been worried about? Could it have played a part in his death? I wondered if Grayson's friend Jeremy might have some ideas, since they'd been coworkers.

I thought about trying to find Jeremy and Luna and asking them for information, but I knew I was going to be seeing them both that night, as long as the play was still on. After overhearing Carol, I had the feeling it would be. She was the determined kind of person who knew how to push things through. I figured I'd head back home, regroup, grab some lunch, and maybe even close my eyes for a few minutes before coming back downtown. It had been a long day so far.

Chapter Three

Although I'd thought I was going to take a short nap, I ended up jolting awake, bleary-eyed and disoriented, when my phone started ringing. An hour and a half had passed by.

Grayson's voice was rueful on the other end. "Hey there. Sorry I woke you up."

I scrubbed at my eyes and tried to become more alert. It was hard when Fitz was curled up on my legs, giving me a sleepily reproachful look. "No worries. I didn't mean to sleep that long. I thought I might just doze off for fifteen minutes or so."

Grayson continued, "I just wanted to let you know the play is on for tonight, after all. Are you still wanting to go with me?"

"Definitely," I said, gently sitting up on the sofa so as not to dislodge Fitz. "I know David was the play's director. Carol was in the staging area at town hall and was saying they were going to honor him during the show. Have you seen or talked to Jeremy?"

"Yeah. The police ended up notifying the family quickly, and Burton got in touch with me to let me know I could identify David in the paper tomorrow. I don't know who started spreading the news, but it seems like everybody knows David was murdered. I'm not even sure who Jeremy heard it from."

I asked, "How did Jeremy take it?"

"He was pretty shaken up to hear what had happened. He kept saying that he just saw David, and he was having a tough time believing he was gone. Jeremy said he and Luna were still planning on being there tonight."

We hung up, and I rubbed Fitz absently for a few minutes. He purred, but kept a watchful eye on me as if thinking I felt a little tense. The nap should have made me feel better, but instead I was groggy and thirsty. I ended up splashing my face with water in the bathroom before making myself a big tumbler of ice water. The hot weather during the parade probably hadn't helped.

Later, I got ready to head out for the play. We decided I'd meet Grayson there since he was still out working on the articles for the next day. The town had a dedicated community theater that put on productions most of the year. Whitby was a small town, but being on a lake in the mountains meant that we also had a fair number of tourists come through. Often they visited the playhouse, too. I had lots of happy memories of seeing plays there with my great-aunt when I was growing up.

Jeremy and Luna were already inside, standing in the aisle with Grayson. Grayson gave me a small smile as I walked up, although he looked a little distracted. Jeremy looked much more somber than he usually did. Ordinarily, he was a sort of happy-go-lucky kind of guy with an easy, laid-back manner and perpetual boyishness. His hair was as tousled as usual, but this time it might have been due to his fingers raking through it, as they were doing right now.

Luna hugged me. "Hey there. Are you okay? I heard you were the one who spotted David."

Jeremy shook his head. "That must have been awful."

I said, "I didn't really know what I was looking at, at first. I thought there might have been a medical emergency or that someone got hurt from a fall." I turned to Jeremy. "I'm so sorry about David. Grayson said the two of you were friends."

Jeremy sighed. "It's more that I'm feeling like I wasn't as good of a friend as I *could* have been, you know? I'd sort of bracketed David firmly into the 'work friend' category. It sounds like he might have had some issues going on in his personal life."

"Did he?" asked Grayson.

Jeremy gave a helpless shrug. "Like I'm saying, I don't know as much as I should. I'm just assuming he probably had personal problems, because of the murder. I don't think that has anything to do with work." He made a face. "At least, I hope not. That would make this all even worse. The cops don't think it was just a random act of violence?"

Grayson said, "Well, they didn't mention that, no. But then, they're not sharing a lot of information with the public right now. I'm sure they probably have to go off the assumption that it was personal."

I said, "Grayson said something about David having an ex-fiancée."

"That's right. David had suddenly broken the engagement. I'm not really sure why. But I know his ex was upset about it. At least, that's what I heard from people at work."

Luna said, "What was her name, Jeremy? Was it somebody we might know?"

"Rebecca somebody. She's a realtor, I think." Jeremy looked up at Grayson. "Actually, she writes a column for the newspaper."

"Oh, sure. Rebecca Thorne. I didn't realize she was dating David," said Grayson. "But then, when we talked, it was usually about her column."

Luna frowned. "I don't remember her column."

Jeremy said in a teasing voice, "Which might be because you don't read the newspaper."

"I do, too!"

"The community events calendar doesn't count," Jeremy said with a mischievous smile. Then he sobered again. "Yeah, David and Rebecca were engaged. But then David broke things off one day, really abruptly. He mentioned it briefly to me, and I didn't press him. It didn't look like he wanted to talk about it. I figured they must have had a major argument or something."

Grayson asked, "Was David in information technology, too?"

"He was in our department, but he was on the project management side of things," said Jeremy. "I helped him meet the rest of the team when he was onboarding."

Patriotic-themed music started playing, a way to nudge the audience to their seats. We found four seats together about midway through the theater. Grayson reached out to hold my hand, squeezing it gently. Luna, on the other side of me, gave me a wink. "You two are so stinkin' cute together," she said.

When the curtains opened, Carol gave a brief speech about David's contribution to the play. "David Hollister believed theater brought the community together. We'd like to dedicate our performance to him tonight. Let's have a moment of silence to remember him."

Men in the audience removed their baseball hats, and everyone bowed their heads, sitting quietly. When it was over, the patriotic music started up again.

"I just saw the guy yesterday," said Jeremy quietly.

Luna said, "I know. It's hard to absorb it, isn't it." She reached out to touch him on the arm.

The curtain opened, and "Yankee Doodle Dandy" reached a crescendo. But no one came out. At first it seemed as if that might be planned, but then seconds kept ticking by with no one appearing. Finally, a flustered-looking Martha Washington hurried onto the stage. She was wearing a long dress and cap and seemed nervous. She launched into a patriotic declaration about freedom and sacrifice to the other women characters, who were there to visit Martha during George's absence (he was apparently enduring the Valley Forge winter).

Grayson whispered to me, "That's David's ex-fiancée Rebecca."

That must have been awkward for both of them after the engagement was broken.

Rebecca definitely seemed stressed, which was totally understandable. Her voice was shaky and it was clear she was forgetting small stage directions. She looked relieved when it was her turn to head offstage, happily yielding her stage time to other actors replicating historical tableaux and giving inspiring patriotic speeches.

After about an hour and a half, the play wrapped up and the actors bowed to applause from the audience. The cast waved and disappeared backstage.

We stood up. Grayson said, "I probably need to talk to Rebecca. I'm going to tell her we can skip her column for the week. I'm sure she must be shaken up over David, and I can fill that space with other content."

I said, "I've met Rebecca before, but I didn't connect her with the Historic Whitby column. Somehow, I envisioned the writer as an elderly lady with her hair in a bun."

Luna raised an eyebrow. "Putting aside her knitting needles to share Whitby's history with eager youngsters?"

"It does sound really cliché when you put it like that," I admitted.

Jeremy said, "I hate to say it, but I'm going to head back home. I'm really wiped." Then he said, "Sorry, Luna. I didn't ask if *you* were ready to go home. Considering we're in the same car and everything."

I knew Luna was definitely a night owl. Her name suited her well. But she said, "You know what, it would probably be good for me to have an early night tonight."

Jeremy said, "One other thing. I think I ought to do something for David's sister, Angela. Maybe I should bring over some flowers or something?" He frowned. "Is that what people do?"

"Maybe some food?" suggested Luna. "Angela could get inundated with flowers. Well, she might get inundated with food too, but at least you can freeze a casserole and eat it later. She has a family, doesn't she?"

Jeremy said, "I think she has a couple of children. Maybe we can go over tomorrow."

Luna shook her head regretfully. "I've got work tomorrow. And I'm not even taking a long lunch break because I swear Wilson has been timing my breaks. He spoke to me about it last week."

Grayson said, "I have the feeling I'm going to be slammed tomorrow with David's death becoming public knowledge. Actually, I'm slammed anyway because I've got staff out on vacation."

I said, "I can go during my lunch break, Jeremy, if you want to head over to Angela's house with me. I know her from the library."

He brightened a little. "That sounds like a good idea." Then his face, always animated, clouded again. "This means we have to cook, doesn't it? I'll admit my cooking ability is rather stunted."

Luna raised an eyebrow. "Are we talking about your usual 'gourmet frozen pizza' with ranch dressing drizzled on top?"

Jeremy looked sheepish. "Hey, it's a perfectly balanced meal. You've got your grains, your dairy, and your vegetables."

"The vegetables being the microscopic bits of dried oregano?" Luna's grin took the sting out of her words.

"Don't knock it until you've tried it," said Jeremy. "Although I suppose bringing Angela a frozen pizza might send the wrong message."

I said, "No cooking needed! We can pick up a fried chicken meal, one of those that has the sides and biscuits included. If you want to pick me up at the library, my lunch break will be at noon."

After we made the plan, Jeremy and Luna headed out. I turned to Grayson. "Mind if I head backstage with you while you talk to Rebecca about her column?"

Grayson quirked an eyebrow at me. "Looking to do some digging?"

I nodded. "Maybe just subtly."

We walked through the door to the backstage area. Rebecca was still in full Martha Washington regalia. She looked absolutely drained and was sitting in a wooden chair while the other actors were getting their stuff to head home. She was an attractive woman in her early thirties with blonde hair and the kind of flawless makeup that probably took significant time each morning.

Rebecca looked up as Grayson and I came closer to her. She gave him a small wave and a brief smile. Grayson introduced me, then said, "Hey, I know it's been a rough day. I just wanted to let you know not to worry about the Historical Whitby column for this week. We've got plenty of extra July Fourth material to run."

Rebecca gave a short laugh. "I'd actually completely forgotten about it, so you weren't going to get it anyway. Can you believe it? I mean, I've been writing that weekly column for the last year or more."

I said, "That's totally understandable. And you did a great job up there tonight. I know how difficult it must have been."

Rebecca looked wryly at me. "I suspect you're telling a white lie, but it's a nice one. Thanks. My head was totally elsewhere. I was missing cues right and left and couldn't remember my lines to save my soul." She paused, looking at Grayson again. "I was just sick over the news about David." A tear escaped, and she brushed it impatiently away.

He said gently, "I know it's got to be really tough to grasp. From everything I've heard about David, he was always so full of life."

"He was. He was the kind of person who always had a lot going on at once and liked it that way," said Rebecca. "Anyway, I'm glad we had the play tonight. David would have wanted it to go on." She gave a little sob at the tail end of the sentence and her shoulders slumped. "You know, I just feel bad about what happened between us. He was everything to me."

Rebecca paused for a few seconds. "It's just such a tragedy. We were starting to work things out between us." She gave a short laugh. "You probably knew about our breakup. The whole town of Whitby did. That's the thing about small towns. Everybody is always in your business."

"You were getting back together?" asked Grayson.

"Well, I'm not totally sure *that* was true. But we were trying to make amends for how our engagement ended. We were at least paving the way toward a friendship, if nothing else. It didn't feel good for either of us to be on bad terms. Plus, in a town the size of Whitby, we were always running into each other. I hated that uncomfortable feeling I had whenever I spotted him. Before, if I saw David downtown, it would always be such a happy moment. We'd end up giving each other a quick hug. Just a second of pure happiness." Rebecca absently pulled a few hairpins out of her elaborate Martha Washington updo. "Did you hear his death is suspicious? Can you believe it?"

Grayson didn't directly answer the question. "Is that what Burton told you?"

Rebecca nodded unhappily. "Yeah. As if David's death wasn't bad enough. Apparently somebody had it in for him. That's the part that's even harder for me to understand. Well, there are a few things I don't get. I can't wrap my head around someone killing him. Plus, who murders somebody in the middle of a crowd?"

But it wasn't really the middle of a crowd. It was behind the crowd. In some ways, if you were bold enough, it was the perfect time and place to kill somebody. Everyone's attention, even the police officers', was directed toward the street and the oncoming parade. There was tons of noise, too, between the music playing from the various floats and the marching band behind me.

"Was David having any trouble with anybody that you're aware of?" I asked. "Personal or professional?"

Rebecca opened her mouth quickly, as if to deny it. But then I saw a thoughtful look cross her features. "Now that you mention it, he and his sister weren't getting along great."

"His sister?" I asked, as if I didn't know her from the library.

She nodded. "Angela is her name. David was always worrying about her, even though I said she was a grown woman and didn't need him fussing over her all the time. He thought she was doing a rotten job raising her kids, apparently. Plus, she wasn't good with budgeting and has all kinds of debt. I guess

Angela didn't appreciate his interference. But David had their best interests at heart."

Then Rebecca stopped short, as if just realizing what she was suggesting. "I'm not saying Angela had anything to do with David's death, though. I know they really cared about each other, and David loved those kids of hers. He was always spending time with them." She gave another short, bitter laugh. "Anyway, the cops think I did it, of course. Right? The ex-fiancée has the best motive of all. But, like I said, David and I loved each other, even if we were going through a rough patch. Nobody understands how complex a relationship can be unless they're in it themselves."

Grayson nodded sympathetically. "You're absolutely right."

"Wait," said Rebecca. "You two are about to get married, aren't you? I totally forgot that. So Ann is your fiancée."

We nodded, and Rebecca gave us a weary smile. "Well, this conversation must have been a downer for you both. Or maybe it's a wake-up call. Remember to keep the people you love close to you. Tell them you love them. Life is short. Sometimes we don't even realize how short it really is until time has totally run out."

A few minutes later, Grayson and I left the Whitby Playhouse. He reached out to hold my hand. "Long day. But you did a great job this morning. I know we've both got a busy day tomorrow. Do you want to try to catch up after work? Look at more wedding magazines and whatnot?"

I glanced at the dispersing crowd, people heading home with their folding chairs and coolers, children still waving small flags. Despite the tragedy, there was something resilient about it all.

"Actually," I said, "what if we picked up a bottle of wine and sat on my porch for a while? We can see the town's fireworks display from there."

Grayson smiled. "That sounds perfect."

An hour later, we were settled on my front porch with a bottle of local wine and two glasses. Fitz was purring contentedly as the summer evening settled around us. The neighborhood was peaceful with kids excitedly waiting for the fireworks and the distant aroma of someone grilling a late supper.

Fitz stretched and resettled himself more comfortably across my lap, as if to say this was exactly where he wanted to spend the rest of the evening.

"Is Fitz all right with fireworks?" asked Grayson, raising an eyebrow.

"Believe it or not, they don't faze him. But then, nothing really does. He's such a laid-back boy."

Just then, a series of bright flashes lit up the sky above us, followed by the deep boom of fireworks. Red, white, and blue sparkles cascades down over the rooftops, and I could hear distant cheers and applause from neighbors who'd stepped outside to watch.

"Perfect timing," Grayson murmured, pulling me closer as another burst of gold and silver painted the night sky.

Fitz opened one disapproving eye at the noise, then seemed to decide the fireworks were acceptable as long as his humans stayed put. He gave a happy sigh.

Chapter Four

After Grayson left, I settled into one of the overstuffed gingham chairs in my sitting room, and Fitz immediately claimed my lap. His purring was therapeutic, but my mind kept churning over the evening's conversations as I ate.

Rebecca's words kept replaying in my head. She almost made it sound like Angela might have been angry enough over what she saw as her brother's interference to murder him. But that description didn't match the Angela I knew from her occasional visits to the library. I remember her as cheerful, hands-on, a bit overwhelmed, but very loving to her family. She was the kind of mom who had a million things going on at one time, but was doing her best to handle them all. Rebecca had said David thought Angela was doing a poor job with the kids. Maybe he was just overly critical because he didn't have children of his own yet and didn't know how hard it was to raise them.

Fitz shifted in my lap, kneading my legs gently as if sensing my restlessness. I absently stroked his fur, trying to reconcile Rebecca's version of Angela with my own observations.

"What do you think, Fitz?" I murmured. "Rebecca made it sound like David was this protective older brother looking out for his irresponsible sister. But something about that doesn't sit right."

Maybe it was because I'd grown up without siblings. My great-aunt had raised me as an only child, so the dynamics Rebecca described felt foreign to me. Was it normal for a brother to be that involved in his adult sister's life? Or was something really wrong with Angela?

Fitz stretched and resettled himself, his purring growing louder. The sound was soothing, but my mind still wouldn't quiet down.

Rebecca had seemed genuinely grief-stricken earlier and perplexed about why someone would want to hurt David. But something nagged at me about her description of their relationship. She'd said they were "working things out," that they'd been trying to "make amends." But then she'd also said David was everything to her, that they loved each other despite going through a rough time.

I said out loud to Fitz, "Those didn't sound like the words of someone casually reconnecting with an ex. They sounded like someone who still harbored serious feelings. Don't you think?"

Fitz opened one eye to look at me, as if to say he was there for me but that our conversation was keeping him from his beauty sleep.

I smiled and gave him another gentle stroke. "You're right. I should probably try to get some sleep too. Tomorrow's going to be another long day."

And hopefully one that would shed some light on David's relationship with his sister.

At work the next morning, I was thinking July 5th might be a quiet day. I figured maybe there were lots of people out of town for the holiday. Instead, business was booming at the library. Moms were there with their kids, our regulars were enjoying reading in our cool air conditioning, and loads of folks were using our computers. They were using our printer and copiers, too, which meant either of those items could glitch at any instant. Our copier in particular often seemed possessed by some unknown malevolent force.

Wilson had been talking on the phone in his office when I arrived, and finally walked out a couple of hours later. He caught me at a fairly quiet moment. "I was hoping I could speak with you for a moment."

I raised an eyebrow. Wilson sounded rather tense. But then, Wilson was always tense, so it was hard to tell. "Absolutely," I said. "What's on your mind?"

"Maybe in my office?" he asked.

Now I was really curious. I didn't think I'd committed any reproachable offenses, so I wasn't totally sure what was on Wilson's mind. I walked into his office, and he closed the door behind me. I saw Luna watching us through the glass windows, her brow crinkled. She made a questioning face at me, and I gave her a shrug. I had no idea what was going on.

Wilson frowned as he noticed Luna's interest. He quickly drew down the shades on the windows and settled at his desk. Naturally, this made me even more perplexed than I'd been before.

"What's with all the subterfuge?" I asked. "Am I in trouble?"

Wilson turned to me with a vague expression. "Pardon? Oh, no, no, nothing like that."

"The library budget? Something with the library board?" Those were two common offenders.

"Hmm?" Wilson asked. "Oh. No, those things aren't currently issues. Well, they are, but not pressing."

"The murder at the parade, then? I didn't actually have anything to do with that, you know. I simply noticed poor David Hollister lying on the floor of the gazebo."

Wilson shook his head. "No." He cleared his throat. "I apologize. I don't seem to be doing the best job introducing this subject."

I was done playing Twenty Questions. Instead, I waited patiently, my hands folded in my lap until Wilson found a way to talk about whatever his issue was.

Finally, he seemed to decide simply to push forward with it. "It's Mona, you see."

"Mona? Is she all right?" I frowned. Luna hadn't mentioned anything being wrong with her mom. "You're not wanting to break up with her, are you?" This would make work incredibly awkward for everyone. Wilson wasn't dating a library employee, of course, but Mona was the next closest thing. Plus, we all loved Mona. Honestly, we all felt a good deal more affection for her than we did for Wilson.

"Certainly not!" said Wilson coldly. "I would never. No, the fact of the matter is that I'm contemplating pursuing more of a bond with Mona."

My eyes widened. "A matrimonial bond?"

Wilson gave a stiff bob of his head. "That is correct."

I sat back in my chair. "Well, that's news, for sure."

Wilson cleared his throat awkwardly. "Ann, I hope you don't mind me asking, but since you've recently been through this yourself . . ." He sighed. "I find myself in need of some advice. I realize this is rather outside the parameter of our usual professional relationship, but I value your judgment, and frankly, I'm not sure who else to turn to."

"Of course! I'd love to help."

Wilson started distractedly reorganizing objects on his desk. "I almost proposed during the festivities yesterday."

"It's probably just as well that you didn't. It didn't end up being a particularly romantic venue, did it?"

"No," agreed Wilson. "I did feel sorry for the young man." He paused. "He wasn't a patron, was he?"

"Not a regular, no. But he works with Jeremy. Jeremy was quite upset about it," I said.

"Ah. Luna's boyfriend. Yes, I'd imagine he would be. A real pity."

I waited. I wasn't at all sure why Wilson had wanted my help. But pumping him for information didn't seem to work especially well. I decided to just sit and wait.

Finally, Wilson moved on. "After some preliminary search engine forays, I discovered that proposing marriage seems to have changed these days. It's morphed into something of an event. It appears that simply possessing the ring is insufficient. There appears to be an entire procedure involved in the proposal process." He said 'procedure' as if he were discussing tax law.

"Procedure?" I asked. I knew what he was getting at, but couldn't resist hearing what his research had turned up.

Wilson pulled out a legal pad covered in his neat handwriting. "According to my internet searches, modern proposals require what's called 'ambiance.' Also something called 'a romantic gesture.' I've compiled a list of options, but I'm concerned about execution. What do you know about the process?"

"The process involved in the proposal itself? People film them and put them on social media. Or they'll tell a friend or family member in advance so they can take pictures and video."

Wilson shuddered, and I hid a smile. There was no way he was going to want to do anything like that. "Tell me what your ideas were. Your list of options."

He handed the legal pad to me.

1. *Restaurant (public, potential embarrassment factor high).*
2. *Lake/other scenic location (weather variables, insect issues)*
3. *Library (familiar territory, but professional boundary concerns)*
4. *Home (private, controllable environment, but lacking romantic ambiance)*
5. *Hot-air balloon (internet suggested, seems mechanically unsound and fairly risky)*

"Wilson," I said gently, "have you considered what Mona would actually enjoy?"

His pen stopped moving, and he frowned.

"Maybe it would be good to think of what makes Mona happy. Or what she enjoys doing," I said.

Wilson's formal expression softened as he considered it. "She likes our morning walks around the town square. And she's always pointing out flowers in people's gardens. She gets excited about small things, like finding a vintage teacup at the flea market last week." His voice grew warmer. "She laughs at my jokes, even the ones that aren't particularly amusing."

"Maybe you should consider some of those elements for your proposal."

Wilson looked genuinely confused. "But where's the ambiance? The internet suggests string quartets or elaborate dinner presentations."

"Don't worry. Mona wouldn't expect a big to-do. Grayson didn't make a big deal out of it, either. It was private and lovely."

For a moment, Wilson seemed as if he might question me about Grayson's proposal. But then he apparently thought better of it. He apparently decided to pursue a slight change of subject. "There is one other matter. The ring itself. I selected it based on practical considerations."

"Price?"

"No, no, not price, per se," said Wilson. "More like appropriate carat weight, a classic setting, and reasonable resale value should circumstances change. But I'm now concerned it's not flashy enough."

"May I see it?"

Wilson opened his desk drawer and removed a velvet box. Inside was a beautiful, classic solitaire. It wasn't huge, but elegant and perfectly suited to Mona's simple, warm style.

"Wilson, it's perfect," I said. "Mona will love it."

"You think so? It's not too understated?"

"It's exactly right. Mona's not a flashy person. This is timeless and elegant, just like she is."

Wilson carefully closed the box. "Very well. I shall propose during one of our walks. Though I might require a practice session."

I hid a smile. "Well, you can try it out on me if you like."

"I'll forgo the part where I kneel, but I shall do that with Mona, of course." He cleared his throat. "Mona," he began formally, "after careful consideration of our relationship trajectory and mutual compatibility factors, I've come to a conclusion."

"Wilson, stop."

He frowned. "Too formal."

"Way too formal. It sounds like you're proposing a merger."

Wilson took a deep breath and tried again. "Mona, these past months with you have been the happiest of my life. You make me laugh, you make me want to be a better person, and you somehow find my organizational systems endearing."

He looked at me, and I nodded encouragingly.

"I can't imagine my future without you in it. Would you do me the tremendous honor of becoming my wife?"

"Perfect," I said, meaning it. "That was beautiful, Wilson."

"It didn't sound too clinical?"

"Not at all. It sounded like you. You and Mona make a wonderful couple. She lights up when you come into a room."

Wilson's face softened when he started thinking about Mona. He seemed momentarily to stop worrying about the execution of the proposal and focus more on the big picture, life with Mona. However, that brief idyll was interrupted by his phone ringing. Looking at it, he frowned. "I'll need to talk with this trustee."

I was heading out the door of his office when he stopped me. "And thanks, Ann."

Luna immediately sauntered up to me. "So? What was that all about? Did Wilson dump another huge project on you?"

I thought about Luna. She was great. But Luna wasn't exactly discreet. Plus, I saw Wilson's face looking out of his office window, his expression alarmed. I gave him what I hoped was a reassuring look.

"No," I said breezily. "Actually, he was just adding on to an existing project."

"Well, that's good," said Luna. "Like I keep saying, Wilson can't just keep expecting you to take on more and more work. You're already putting in far more time at the library than you need to. You have a life! You're planning a wedding. But he always expects more and more."

Although this wasn't what had happened in this particular instance, it was still true. Wilson was fond of assigning me to pet projects. One issue, though, was that Wilson had so many pet projects. "I think he *can* keep expecting more," I answered. "I haven't really seen any sign of that abating."

Luna wagged her finger at me. "The problem is that you do a phenomenal job with the stuff he sends your way. Instead, you should be sloppy with it."

"Sloppy?"

"Yeah," said Luna. "Don't finish a project. Don't even *think* about the project. Basically, just totally fail."

"I have the feeling I'm not wired that way."

Luna snorted. "Then rewire yourself. Otherwise, Wilson is going to keep dumping stuff on you." She suddenly changed course, which was a very Luna thing to do. I'd gotten used to her non sequiturs and abrupt conversational detours, but it could still be very jarring. "Now, when is my boyfriend coming to take you on your lunch date?"

I chuckled. "Jeremy is coming in ten minutes to take me over to see Angela."

"Excellent." Luna turned as the library doors opened, raising her eyebrows in surprise. "Well, well! Looks like he's come early. He must be eager to hang out with you."

But that apparently wasn't the reason for Jeremy's early arrival. Instead, it seemed to do with his anxiety about getting the food over to Angela and returning me back to the library in a timely fashion, as he quickly explained.

Luna smiled at me. "Doing bereavement visits is a bit out of Jeremy's wheelhouse."

"I want to do a good job," said Jeremy eagerly. "And I don't really feel very awkward about offering condolences. The thing is that I haven't been to pick up fried chicken before. I don't know where the fried chicken place is. Honestly, I don't even *eat* fried chicken."

Considering how laid-back Jeremy ordinarily was, he was quite keyed up about taking a simple takeout meal to a former colleague's grieving sister.

I said, "We have it all under control. I called ahead earlier and ordered the food. It'll be ready when we get there. And I've mapped the route to Angela's house on my phone. We're good to go."

Jeremy looked relieved. "Okay. Whew. Let's head on out, then. I've been trying to figure out what I'm going to say to Angela. Maybe I'll come up with something on the way over."

I had the feeling this was the first time someone in Jeremy's life, however tangential, had passed away. I said, "We'll just tell her we're so sorry. Then, if you like, I can do most of the talking."

"That sounds perfect, Ann," said Jeremy with alacrity.

Luna gave us a wave as she headed back to the children's department. "Good luck, you two."

I hopped into Jeremy's car, and we set off. "It's right down near the shoe repair shop," I told him.

Jeremy looked surprised. I couldn't tell if it was because he didn't realize the chicken place was that close, or whether it was because the town had a shoe repair shop. It turned out it was the latter. "Shoe repair," he said slowly.

"Yes."

He frowned as he drove in that direction. "Wasn't there a name for a job like that?"

"A cobbler."

Jeremy's eyebrows raised, which made his frowning face rather ferocious-looking. "Like a peach cobbler."

"Spelled the same but quite different." I gave him a wry smile. "You seem sort of stunned."

"I sure am. I had no idea that was still a way to make a living."

I said, "Of course it is. I've gone there regularly to get shoes repaired. What do you do when your shoes start falling apart?"

"I buy new ones," he said simply.

"Ah. Well, IT pays better than being a librarian, I suppose."

Jeremy said in a mulling tone, "Although it's kind of wasteful, isn't it? Maybe I need to look into using the shoe repair place." He gave it a considering look as he slowly drove by.

Angela's house was in one of Whitby's older neighborhoods, a modest two-story with a small front yard that looked like it had been recently mowed but could use some attention to the flower beds. A practical older-model Honda minivan sat in the driveway next to a newer-looking mountain bike that had been carelessly tossed in the grass.

Angela answered the door wearing dark slacks and a wrinkled blouse, as if she'd started dressing professionally, but hadn't quite finished the process. Her shoulder-length brown hair was pulled back into a ponytail, and she had the slightly frazzled look of someone trying to hold too many things together.

"Jeremy!" she said at once. She looked at me with a quizzical expression on her face. Before I could introduce myself, she said, "Ann? From the library, right?" She looked down at the large bags of food from the fried chicken place and teared up. "Oh gosh. I'm sorry. This is so sweet of you both. I keep crying when people are kind to me. Please, come on inside."

Chapter Five

The living room showed signs of a family in constant motion. There were real estate flyers from Angela's work scattered across the coffee table next to what looked like summer job applications, a driver's permit study guide, and some college brochures. A basket of unfolded laundry occupied one chair, and there were several coffee mugs and soft drinks that appeared to have been abandoned mid-sip. She thanked us again, taking the large bag of food and hurrying off to the kitchen to stick it in the fridge.

I glanced at the property listings. So Angela worked in real estate. But Rebecca Thorne was also a real estate agent. In a town the size of Whitby, they probably knew each other, at least professionally. That had to make David's broken engagement even more awkward for everyone involved.

Angela returned from the kitchen seconds later and ran a hand through her hair, forgetting there was a ponytail. She pulled some strands loose from her hair tie. "Can I get you something to eat? Or drink?"

We both shook our heads as Angela continued with a shaky laugh. "This place is a total disaster. Here, let me clear off a place for you to sit." She swept the laundry basket off the chair, setting it down on the floor. A dog of indeterminate heritage came in to investigate the laundry basket before looking disinterested and loping away. Jeremy and I took our seats.

Angela said, "It's so incredibly thoughtful for you to have brought food. It's been impossible to keep to any kind of a schedule or routine at all. I keep meaning to eat something, but then I forget or the phone rings, or something else comes up."

As if to illustrate her point, a teenage boy appeared in the living room doorway, wearing large headphones around his neck and an expression of carefully controlled grief. "Hey," he said gruffly to his mother, "I'm going to head over to Uncle David's place to get my skateboard."

Angela looked stricken. "Tyler, you can't go over right now."

He raised his chin. "I need to get it."

"Yes, but I don't know . . . well, the police have been over there. I think they have his house blocked off still."

Tyler drooped, and I could see Angela searching for the words to make everything okay again, even though there really weren't any. While she was still looking for them, Tyler pivoted and darted up the stairs, his face stormy.

Angela gave us a tight smile. "That was my son," she said sadly. "He and David were pretty close. Both my kids were. He was great with them." She sat down heavily in a chair that was full of clutter, unmindful of it.

Jeremy said gently, "I bet he must have been an awesome uncle. David talked about your kids at work sometimes. I could tell he really cared about them."

Emotions flickered across Angela's features. I could see a bit of gratitude, but there seemed to be something else there, too, that I couldn't quite name. "Oh, he cared, all right. Sometimes he cared just a little too much." She immediately looked stricken. "That came out wrong. I didn't mean it to sound that way."

"Don't apologize," I said gently. "Family relationships are always complicated."

She looked relieved. "Thank you. Tyler and David were especially close. David was the fun uncle, you know. He'd actually go skateboarding with Tyler, if you can believe it." A small, sad smile crossed her face. "I told David I'd break my neck if I tried to skateboard, which wouldn't help anybody. But Tyler loved having someone who'd actually get on a board with him."

Angela added quietly, "Tyler confided in David more than he confides with me these days. You know how teenagers are. But David had his ear in a way I don't anymore."

I said, "I'm sure that's totally normal. And it's great Tyler had somebody he could talk to."

"Oh, it was," said Angela. "Everybody keeps telling me how great David was and how much he loved his family." She absentmindedly picked up one of the abandoned empty coffee mugs before setting it back down again. "And he totally did. No question. But he also had very strong opinions about how I should be raising my kids, spending my money, and living my life."

Jeremy shifted in his seat, looking uncomfortable. It was probably hard for him to square this version of David with the guy he knew at work.

I said to Angela, "That must have been really difficult."

She nodded. "It was tough. I got divorced three years ago and felt like I was starting everything over from scratch. I haven't gotten any real support from my ex-husband, either, so it's all been pretty hard. David was a saint, though. He moved here from Charlotte and told me he wanted to help."

Jeremy brightened at Angela's words. He clearly felt more comfortable when David was getting kudos from his sister for doing a good job. "That's awesome that he did that," said Jeremy cheerfully.

"Yeah," continued Angela. "He did help, don't get me wrong. But at some point, it started feeling less like help and more like . . . supervision."

"Oh," said Jeremy."

I said, "I know yesterday was awful for you, Angela. I'm so sorry."

She gave a short laugh. "It was pretty bad. Of course, I was volunteering at the festival, too. My real estate office was encouraged to help with the event; they like us to engage with the community. So I was there all day with, of course, Rebecca." She winced. "You might not know this, but David had recently ended his engagement to Rebecca."

Jeremy looked miserable again. "I did know that. Wow, that must have made you feel uncomfortable working with Rebecca after that."

"It was. But honestly, it's been uncomfortable for plenty of reasons. She's been acting strange for weeks, even before the end of the engagement."

"Strange how?" I asked.

Angela said, "She'd pump me for information about properties. And she kept wanting to know things that weren't really her business. On top of it all, she kept bringing David up. Rebecca was totally fishing for information."

"What kind of information?" asked Jeremy, his forehead scrunching into a frown.

"Money stuff. Family business. She asked me last week if David seemed worried about anything." Angela gave another humorless laugh. "I told Rebecca that David was always worried about something. Usually me."

I could hear a door open and close upstairs, followed by footsteps. A girl who looked to be around seventeen appeared at the top of the stairs, wearing a Whitby High tee-shirt. Like her brother, she also looked drained and worried.

"Hey, Mom." The girl stopped short when she saw Jeremy and me. "Oh, sorry. I didn't know you had company."

"Emma, these are David's friends from work. They brought us lunch. Or supper, whichever you want."

Emma's face softened. "That's really nice. Thanks." She looked at her mother with concern in her eyes. "You've been eating, right? Did you have breakfast?"

"I'm fine honey," said Angela without answering the question.

Emma clearly didn't believe this, but didn't push. "I'll grab some food later. I'm heading over to Fran's house, if that's okay. I'm bringing a bag in case I end up sleeping over there."

"That's okay," said Angela.

After Emma left, Angela sighed. "She's been staying at friends' houses a lot lately, even before David died. Emma switches back and forth between hovering over me, worried I'm not eating or sleeping enough, and then wanting to totally escape the whole situation."

"That sounds like a lot of pressure for a seventeen-year-old," I said.

"It is. Emma's always been mature for her age, though, and really observant." Her voice grew thoughtful. "Actually, a couple of weeks ago, she told me he seemed really preoccupied. She could tell he was worried about something, but when she asked him about it, he just said everything was fine."

Jeremy leaned forward slightly. "Did Emma have any idea what might have been bothering him?"

"No. I just assumed it was regarding his breakup with Rebecca, but Emma wasn't so sure." Angela sighed. "Anyway, now both kids are looking for ways to stay distracted and not think about David being gone. They both loved spending time at his house. He had the big-screen TV, the gaming setup, and all the snacks they liked. It made this house seem pretty boring in comparison." There was hurt in her voice.

"He sounds like a fun uncle, but nothing beats mom," I said.

Jeremy added, "I'm sure the kids know you're doing your best."

"David didn't always think so." Angela's words came out in a rush. "He had opinions about their screen time, their curfews, and their grades. He thought I was way too lenient." She gave a helpless shrug. "Over at his house, he wouldn't let them play games or stream movies until their homework was done. He meant well, you know. But sometimes it made it feel like he thought I was failing them."

I said, "That sounds really hard."

Angela's eyes filled with tears again at my sympathetic tone. One trickled out, and she dashed it away with a quick brush of her hand. "The really awful thing is that we had a fight about it just last week. The back-to-school sales have started, even though school isn't back for another month or more. Tyler wanted to shop the sales, and I guess he told David about it. David offered to take him shopping." She paused, then sighed. "I just lost it. That was one of the few things I liked doing with the kids. When it comes to spending money, I mean. There's something about getting those new backpacks and notebooks and stuff that I love. It's like a fresh beginning."

I knew exactly what she was talking about. But then, I'd always had a soft spot for going to an office supply store. I could spend more money getting pens, notebooks, and sticky notes than getting shoes or other clothes.

Angela took a deep breath as she continued. "I didn't handle it well, and David ended up getting offended. He said I was just being stubborn and that he could afford the shopping trip better than I could. I should have let it drop, but it hurt my feelings. I went off on him." She rubbed her eyes again.

She gestured around the living room with its mix of hand-me-down furniture and worn upholstery. "David meant well. He really did care about us. But he'd fuss when I'd spend money on anything he thought was unnecessary. Like when I bought Emma a nice coat for Christmas last year. It wasn't that expensive, but it was nicer than what we usually buy. He thought I should have asked him to buy it for Emma." Her voice grew tired. "I mean, look around. It's not like I'm throwing money around. Everybody can tell I'm not exactly living it up here."

"Angela, I'm so sorry," said Jeremy somberly. "But you know David knew you loved him. And he loved all of you. You were family."

"I hope so. I really hope so," she said in a small voice. Then she took a trembling breath. "It's just been terrible. Having David just unexpectedly ripped away from everybody who loved him. Then the cops were asking me all kinds of questions."

"Burton?" I asked.

She shook her head. "No, this was somebody with the state police. I wish it *had* been Burton. He actually knows me and the kind of person I am. He knows I'm not a murderer."

Jeremy looked shocked. "They couldn't have thought you had anything to do with David's passing."

"Couldn't they? The cops didn't seem to have gotten that memo. They demanded that I give them an alibi for when David was murdered. I told them I was volunteering at the festival, and they seemed to think this meant I killed my brother." The last couple of words turned into a sob. Angela struggled to regain control.

I hesitated for a moment, then gently asked, "Angela, can you think of anyone who might have wanted to hurt David? Someone the police might be looking at?"

Angela's face tightened. "Rebecca," she said without hesitation. "I mean, I hate to say that, but she's the obvious person, isn't she?"

"Because of the broken engagement?" asked Jeremy.

"Exactly. You don't know how uncomfortable it's been at work since they broke up. We're both trying to avoid each other, which is pretty hard in a tiny office." Angela shifted in her chair. "Rebecca's been really quiet and withdrawn around me. Before the breakup, she was always chatty and wanting to collaborate on listings. Now she barely makes eye contact."

"Did David tell you anything about why they ended things?" I asked.

Angela shook her head. "David wasn't one to share personal details, especially when it came to relationship problems. All he said was he'd realized they weren't compatible." She paused. "But Rebecca's been throwing herself into work since then. She's been dealing with some big developer from out of town. I don't know all the details, but it seems like a major deal for her."

After that, Angela shifted the subject to more immediate concerns. Angela talked about trying to arrange the memorial service on short notice, dreading the phone call she still needed to make to their mother in Florida, and wondering how to handle David's house and belongings. She kept circling back to practical worries, hoping the kids would be okay, wondering how to help them process their grief, and whether she should have them talk with someone.

"The guidance counselor at school offered to meet with them over the summer," Angela said. "I keep going back and forth on whether that's a good idea or if it would make things worse."

Jeremy shifted uncomfortably, clearly out of his depth with discussions about teenage grief counseling. I could see him glance longingly at the door.

"It might be worth trying," I said. "Sometimes it helps kids to talk with someone outside the family."

Angela nodded, looking exhausted. "I just want to do right by them. David said I worried too much, but how do you not worry when something like this happens?"

A few minutes later, Jeremy and I exchanged glances and began making our exit noises. We thanked Angela again, reminding her to call if she needed anything.

Chapter Six

Jeremy and I sat in his car for a moment before he started the engine.

"I don't think I knew David as well as I thought I did," he said finally.

"None of us really know what happens behind closed doors in a family."

Jeremy was quiet again for a few moments. "I'd hate to think Angela had anything to do with what happened to David. You don't think she lashed out, do you? She was mad at him. She'd actually *just* had a big blow-up with him. Angela was volunteering at the festival, she said, so she would have been nearby."

I thought about how Angela was angry about how pushy David was on raising her children, and how Tyler and Emma both seemed very close to their uncle. And I had to wonder if David, a single man, would have left his estate to his sister in the case of his death. Angela had mentioned that money was tight.

"I don't know," I said honestly. "But there seemed to be a lot going on under the surface in their family. It's tough to say."

Jeremy started up the car. "Want to run by a fast-food place to grab lunch and take it to the library with you?"

"Actually, could you drop me off at the coffee shop? They have sandwiches there, and I can get coffee at the same time. I feel like I'm going to start dragging this afternoon unless I get some caffeine."

Ten minutes later, I was walking out of Keep Grounded toward the library with a bagged BLT sandwich and a large coffee. I spotted Rebecca at an outdoor table at a restaurant a few doors down. She was sitting with a silver-haired, expensively dressed man. Judging from the papers scattered on the table, it seemed to have been a business meeting.

Their interaction caught my attention. Rebecca was leaning forward in an almost deferential pose as she spoke. There was something about her body language with the way she tilted her head and her overly bright smile that seemed calculated to please.

I lingered for a moment, pretending to check my phone as I caught fragments of their conversation.

". . . absolutely fascinating history," Rebecca was saying, her voice carrying that enthusiastic tone she'd used in her Martha Washington performance. "Everything we've uncovered really brings the past to life. Your clients will feel like they're not just buying a home, but becoming stewards of American heritage."

The silver-haired man leaned back in his chair, clearly pleased by what he was hearing. "That's exactly the kind of narrative my buyers are looking for. They want properties with real stories, real soul."

Rebecca's smile grew even brighter. "I'm so grateful you're willing to work with local agents like me. I know you could easily handle these sales through your own channels."

There was something almost performative about her enthusiasm that made it seem as if she were playing another role. Now she was the eager local expert sharing precious historical secrets.

The man picked up one listing, studying it carefully. "Underground Railroad, you said? That's quite significant."

"Isn't it? The hidden passages and the documented stops are all there in the family records."

The man seemed increasingly interested as Rebecca continued her pitch, occasionally nodding or making notes. She was clearly in her element, pulling out documents and beaming.

Then, wanting to make sure I was back at the library with some time to eat my lunch, I hurriedly passed them. I wondered if the man was the out-of-town developer Angela had mentioned Rebecca spending so much time with.

I was home from work and had just finished feeding Fitz when I heard Grayson's car in the driveway. Through the kitchen window, I could see him gathering what looked like newspapers and a laptop bag from his passenger seat.

Fitz meowed a greeting as Grayson came in the front door, immediately winding around his ankles in that persistent way cats have when they really want attention.

"Hey there, buddy," Grayson said, reaching down to scratch behind Fitz's ears. "Good to see you."

After Fitz allowed Grayson to move, Grayson pulled me into a hug that lasted longer than usual. "How are you holding up? Jeremy told me the visit with Angela was pretty intense."

"It was," I admitted. "I felt bad for Angela, too. She obviously really loved her brother, and her kids were crazy about him. But she'd also thought he was too involved in how she was raising Emma and Tyler. They had a big argument not long before he died. Now that he's gone, she's feeling guilty."

Grayson said, "That's tough. Of course, she had no idea he was going to be murdered. But guilt isn't really rational, is it?" He walked over to the coffee table and hesitated. "Do you mind if I spread some stuff out? I brought some work home."

"Of course." I settled into my favorite gingham chair while Grayson arranged newspapers and printouts on the table. Fitz immediately claimed the stack of papers closest to him, settling on top with a satisfied purr.

"Research of some kind?" I tried to peer around Fitz, who was now happily rolling on his back in the papers.

"Sort of." Grayson eased Fitz to his lap, where the orange and white cat appeared pleased to have achieved his actual goal. "I was thinking about our conversation with Rebecca after the play. I ended up going back through Rebecca's recent 'Historic Whitby' newspaper columns."

I raised an eyebrow. "Looking for what?"

"I'm not totally sure. I guess I was just trying to get a better sense of who Rebecca was. Sometimes you can get that from a person's writing style." Grayson gave me a grin. "I guess I don't have to tell you that. You're the librarian."

"You're right, though. You can get into a writer's head through their words. It makes sense to re-read Rebecca's columns and see if you get a different angle on her."

Grayson nodded. "Right. Except I found something else, instead of her writing voice. Rebecca's been writing about different properties for sale and some of her historical details seem sort of creative."

"Creative how?"

Grayson showed me a column from a few weeks ago. "Like this one about the Victorian house on Elm Street. Rebecca wrote about how it was supposedly a stop on the Underground Railroad, with hidden passages and secret rooms. Of course, the place has been remodeled a ton of times, so there's nothing like that there now."

I skimmed through the column. It reminded me of what I'd overheard today after I'd gotten my coffee downtown. "That's a huge historical claim. Did she site sources?"

"That's what caught my attention. She mentions 'newly discovered historical documents' but doesn't say where they came from or who found them."

I raised my eyebrows. "That seems kind of suspect."

"Right. I called the historical society this afternoon to ask about these new discoveries. They had no record of any new documents coming to light recently."

Fitz stretched and resettled himself in Grayson's lap, as if he found our conversation mildly interesting, but not worth losing sleep over.

"So Rebecca is either working with sources the historical society doesn't know about," I said slowly, "or she's embellishing property histories."

Grayson said, "I'm wondering if it's the latter. Is she embellishing histories because these are homes she's listing or that she's about to list? After all, a property with Underground Railroad connections would be worth significantly more than just a nice old house. Is she trying to create a market for historical properties? Maybe she's working with outside buyers who'd pay premium prices for them?"

We sat quietly for a moment, with Fitz's contented purring the only sound. Outside, the summer evening was settling into that peaceful time when the humidity and jarring heat of the day finally start easing up.

"What do you make of all this?" asked Grayson.

I considered the question for a minute. "It's hard to say. Maybe Rebecca just got a couple of her properties mixed up. She has a lot going on, after all. She recently had a broken engagement. Then David died. Maybe she made an honest mistake."

"Or maybe she didn't," said Grayson. "Maybe David found out about the scam, broke their engagement, and threatened to blow the whistle."

"True." I reached over to stroke Fitz, who opened one green eye to acknowledge my attention. "I did overhear Rebecca talking to a guy who might have been a developer at a restaurant downtown today. She was talking about a house with Underground Railroad connections. It might have been the same one in the article."

Grayson frowned. "I hope she's not making things up. Especially if it's getting printed in the paper. I mean, usually I don't have to worry too much about fabrication for *The Whitby Times*. Now I'm wondering if I've got to start doing a lot of fact-checking."

He shifted and then abruptly changed the subject. "What did you think of Angela overall, during your visit with Jeremy today?" asked Grayson

"She seemed like somebody who has her hands full. Angela was worried about helping her kids go through the grieving process, and then is juggling working and her own grief. It seemed like a lot."

Grayson said, "Jeremy was saying that Angela was upset about David trying to give her parenting advice or something."

"Apparently, David had been offering his opinion on stuff like screen time. It didn't sound like Angela appreciated it too much. Rebecca made it sound like David was this protective brother looking out for his irresponsible sister, but Angela strikes me as competent and overwhelmed, not irresponsible. And now we know Rebecca might not be the most reliable narrator with factual details. At least, if she's making up stuff for the paper."

Grayson gently put Fitz on the floor, where the cat padded off toward the kitchen. Then Grayson moved from the sofa to the arm of my chair, close enough that I could lean against him. "So what do we do about all this?"

"Keep our eyes open, I guess. And try to figure what David was worried about before his death. Angela mentioned that even her daughter had noticed David seemed anxious and preoccupied."

Grayson said, "Good point. I had several people mention to me today that David had seemed distracted lately. Not just with opening night nerves for the play, but really worried about something."

"Angela said the same thing," I murmured.

Grayson was quiet for a few moments. Then he said, "You know, it occurs to me that we're spending lots of time talking about murder and family drama."

I smiled. "Are you suggesting we change the subject?"

"Well, we do have a wedding to plan. And a house to potentially expand." He gestured toward his laptop bag. "I actually brought those architectural drawings with me again. Thought maybe we could make some decisions that don't involve investigating suspicious deaths." Grayson walked over to retrieve the papers, spreading them out on the coffee table.

I laughed, feeling some of the day's tension fade. "That sounds like an excellent idea. Though I should warn you that Fitz has very strong opinions about the sunroom addition."

As if summoned, Fitz reappeared from the kitchen, which he'd double-checked to ensure there was no morsel left overlooked in his food bowl. He quickly positioned himself directly on top of the architectural drawings.

"See?" I said with a laugh. "He's already claiming his space."

Grayson chuckled, carefully moving Fitz so we could look at the plans. "Well, at least one of us knows what he wants. You and I have been pretty indecisive."

We spent the next hour going over the drawings, chatting about the merits of different room layouts and discussing where our combined book collections might live. Finally, Fitz, apparently deciding we'd spent enough time on boring human concerns, clambered into my lap, purring loudly enough to drown out further conversation about either murder or home renovation.

"I think that's Fitz's way of saying we've done enough for one day," I said.

Grayson gathered up his papers and plans. "He's probably right. Some problems are better solved with a good night's sleep."

Chapter Seven

The next morning, I'd barely gotten settled at the reference desk when I heard the familiar sound of Zelda Smith's voice rising above the typical library murmuring. Zelda was my neighbor, a woman in her sixties with henna-colored red hair. She usually spent the time when she wasn't working reception at a local mechanic by monitoring HOA violations, volunteering at the library, and trying to recruit people for various neighborhood committees. What was unusual today was the rhythmic *crack, crack, crack* accompanying her words.

Curious, I walked over to see what was happening. Zelda was sitting at a study table with Owen, both of them surrounded by a stack of books about smoking cessation. She had an industrial-sized bag of sunflower seeds beside her and was methodically working through them, adding shells to a neat pile on a napkin.

"Owen, hand me that book on the bottom shelf, would you? Can't read the fine print from here. Stupid publishers putting tiny font on covers."

Owen, the boy the library had practically adopted as its own, stooped down to retrieve the book. "This one? On hypnosis?" He looked pleased to be helpful.

"That's the one," grated Zelda in her cigarette-ruined voice. "Day four of not smoking, so I'm trying every trick in the book." She cackled. "Literally. The doctor says I need to keep my mouth busy. Sunflower seeds are better than toothpicks, and definitely better than those nasty nicotine gums, I'll give you that."

"Zelda?" I said, settling into a chair across from them. "You're quitting smoking? That's awesome!"

Owen beamed. "She's doing great, too."

A mulish expression crossed Zelda's features, and she snorted. "Don't sound so surprised, Ann. Just because I've been smoking for forty years doesn't mean I can't stop when I want to." She cracked another sunflower seed. "Though I'll tell you what. That printer Wilson refuses to replace picked a rotten time to start screeching again. Makes me want to light up a whole pack just to spite it."

"Are your lungs feeling better?" I asked. "How are you feeling overall?"

"Cranky as a wet cat," she answered promptly. Her expression softened slightly as she glanced at Owen. "But this one's been keeping me honest. Although he did make me a gold chart like I'm in kindergarten." She gave the boy a gruff but approving look. "Works better than you'd think."

Owen grinned. "Miss Zelda gets a gold star for every day without cigarettes."

I had to smile at the mental image of Zelda Smith, neighborhood watchdog and HOA stickler, earning gold stars on a chart created by a ten-year-old. "Hey, that's a great system. I love it," I said.

Luna materialized from the children's section and appeared to have overheard at least part of our conversation. Our library teen, Timothy, joined us too, likely curious over our little gathering. "You've quit smoking? Wow, Zelda! Woo-hoo!"

"Don't jinx it," said Zelda, scowling, though there was no real heat in the scowl. "It's only been four days. Let's see what I'm doing in four months."

Timothy said, "My mom quit a couple of years ago. She said the first week was bad, but then it got easier."

"I certainly hope so," Zelda said as she added another sunflower shell to her pile. "Owen's been helping me stay accountable. Do you know how much time he's spending volunteering?"

"I do," I said. "Timothy's been mentoring him with our tech programs, too."

"Owen's a natural," said Timothy with a shrug. "He figured out the new checkout system faster than the staff did."

Owen's face flushed with pride.

Wilson emerged from his office looking harried. "Ann, I don't suppose you could—" He stopped short when he saw our group gathered around the study table. "Ms. Smith. You're not eating in the library?"

Zelda fixed him with a steely look. "The food is medicinal, Wilson. Doctor's orders. Do you want me to quit smoking or not?"

Wilson looked as if he was carefully weighing the relative merits of someone eating versus someone smoking, and clearly decided the seeds were the lesser evil. "Well, congratulations on your health journey." He turned to me. "Ann, I understand we're having some integration issues with the summer reading program database that I'd like someone to look at."

Luna broke in. "Wilson," she said in her relentlessly cheerful way, "maybe save the tech crisis when we're done celebrating Zelda's achievement? Four smoke-free days is a big deal."

"Of course, of course," murmured Wilson absently, his brain obviously still focused on the integration issue.

Zelda looked gratified. "It's early days yet. But I'm feeling hopeful." She gathered up her shells into a small paper bag she'd apparently brought for that purpose. "Owen, would you help me return my books? Not the hypnosis one, though. I think I got all the good stuff out of the others."

Luna and I walked away. She turned to me with a grin. "Did you ever think you'd see the day when Zelda Smith would be getting life coaching from a kid?"

"Never in a million years," I admitted. "But it's pretty sweet."

"It sure is." Luna glanced around to make sure we had some privacy. "Hey, Jeremy was telling me about the trip you both took to see Angela. How did you think that went? Because Jeremy was pretty confused about the whole thing."

"Ah. Probably because he heard about a different version of David from Angela."

Luna nodded. "Right."

"Well, it was Angela's perspective. Of course, a sister is going to have a different point-of-view than a colleague at work. Rebecca had made it sound like Angela was kind of irresponsible as a parent and that David was stepping in. But it seemed more complicated than that."

Luna said, "I figured. Nothing is all that simple, is it?"

"Angela made it sound more like David was butting in. She seemed kind of hurt that he thought she was doing a poor job monitoring the kids' screen time and stuff like that. But Angela is a single mom of teens. She's working hard at what seems like a very busy job. So maybe it's more a matter of her doing her best and David, who didn't have kids, not knowing what it's really like to be a parent."

Luna said, "Sounds likely. Okay, well, I was just curious. Jeremy was kind of in a funk last night, and you know how chipper he usually is. He was wondering whether Angela killed her brother because he was interfering. I told him it was too early to know that. That there were other leads."

I perked up. "Do you know of any? Besides Rebecca and Angela, I mean?"

"Maybe. My mom was at the community center last week after Wilson dropped her off for some kind of senior event Whitby was putting on. Anyway, she was telling me Janet McKenzie was there running a theater camp for kids."

"I remember Janet," I said. "She's the new drama teacher at the high school, right?"

"Right. When Carol Winters retired, Janet stepped into her job. Anyway, like I said, she's running this summer theater camp." Luna lowered her voice. "Mom said Janet was worked up about David last week. Janet auditioned for the Martha Washington part in *The Spirit of '76* play. You know, the role Rebecca ended up playing."

"Oh, gotcha. So Janet had hurt feelings that David chose Rebecca for the part over her." It sounded like low-level resentment to me. Not really something to murder someone over.

Luna said, "Judging from what my mom said, it was more than just sour grapes. Apparently, David told Janet to 'stick to teaching kids' when she auditioned for the play."

"Wow. I bet that created some bad feelings."

"I'll say," said Luna. "From what I heard, Janet went on and on about it. Of course, Janet *is* a theater teacher. Maybe she's a little dramatic in real life."

Before I could respond, my phone buzzed with a text message. I glanced at it. It was a message from Grayson asking if I wanted to grab a bite after work.

"Everything good?" asked Luna. It was a valid question, since I suddenly realized I'd been frowning as I thought things through.

"It's all good. Grayson was just asking about supper." I looked up at Luna. "I think I'd like to talk to Janet. Do you think she'd be at the community center with her camp? It sounds like one of those things where the kids stay there instead of going on field trips around town, right?"

"Probably. Mom said they were practicing to put on a play for their families at the end of the week."

I quickly texted Grayson back to see if he wanted to visit the theater camp with me and grab lunch instead of dinner. But his response came back almost immediately. He was swamped, but asked if I could take some photos at the camp for the paper's social media.

"Looks like I'm going to visit Janet solo. But at least I have an excuse to be there now." I showed Luna the text.

"Good timing," said Luna. "Don't you have lunch now?"

I frowned, looking at my watch. "Wow, I've really lost track of time this morning."

"Grab your purse and go! And remember to actually eat something while you're out."

As I headed for the door, I heard Zelda's voice again, this time from the circulation desk where she was checking out the hypnosis book. "Owen, remind me to list today's activities in my quit journal when I get home. I've had *minimal* cravings today." Then, a sunflower seed cracked.

The community center was full of activity when I arrived. It looked like they were sponsoring a talk by a local gardener, an aerobics class, and the theater camp Janet was giving. I had my phone camera ready for the photos Grayson requested. I could hear voices and music coming from the main room, along with what sounded like furniture being moved around.

I followed the noise and looked into a big multipurpose room that had been transformed into a makeshift theater space. About fifteen kids ranging from elementary school to high school were scattered around. Some of them were practicing lines, others were painting backdrops, and a few looked like they were working on costumes.

In the middle of everything was a woman I recognized as Janet McKenzie. She was just as I remembered from seeing her around town—in her forties with graying hair pulled back in a messy bun and wearing paint-splattered clothes that somehow managed to look intentionally artistic instead of accidentally messy. She was directing a group of middle school students who were trying to position a sizeable piece of plywood painted to look like a building.

"Move it a little to the left," Janet called out. "Okay, perfect! Now let's see how it looks with the lighting."

I stepped into the room and waited for a break in the action to explain why I was there. One of the older students noticed me first.

"Ms. McKenzie, there's somebody here," the girl said.

Janet turned, and I could see her trying to place me.

Chapter Eight

"Ann Beckett," I said, walking forward with a smile. "From the library. I hope I'm not interrupting anything too important."

"Oh, of course!" Janet's face brightened. "The parade grand marshal, in the flesh. What brings you here?"

"Grayson Phillips from the *Whitby Times* asked if I could take some pictures of local summer programs for their social media. A community interest sort of story. Is it okay if I snap a few photos?" Then I frowned, remembering sometimes there was paperwork that came along with publishing pictures of minors. "Do I need to ask their parents to sign something?"

Janet said, "Ordinarily, yes, but I had photography permission on one of the release forms for the camp. So fire away! They'll all be delighted to see pictures from drama camp. We're preparing for our family showcase at the end of the week. The kids have been working so hard."

I started taking photos, capturing the kids at work on their different projects. "Your camp looks amazing. What a great way to keep kids occupied during the summer."

"That's the idea," said Janet, with a smile. "I want theater to be accessible to everybody, not just the kids whose parents can afford private lessons. Those are taught by the established theater crowd and aren't cheap."

There was an edge in her voice during the last bit. It made me lower my phone. "The established theater crowd?"

"Oh, you know. The people who've been running things around Whitby the same way for years. Sometimes it's tough for new ideas to get a fair hearing."

One of the younger campers tugged on Janet's shirt. "Ms. McKenzie, the soldier hat doesn't fit."

"Oh, one second, honey, I'll fix it." Janet walked over to help adjust the costume while I continued taking pictures. When she came back, I decided to try to shift the subject to July Fourth.

"Did you have your campers over the Fourth? I think I remember seeing them lined up for the parade."

Janet said, "It's a two-week camp, so we were in session. We had a float with scenes from American history. I was so proud of the kids' hard work. Of course, it ended up being a tough day for other reasons."

"Because of what happened to David Hollister?"

"Partly." Janet picked up a paintbrush and absently cleaned it with a rag, although it didn't seem to need any cleaning. She sighed. "I mean, I'm sorry about what happened to him, of course. But David and I had some unfinished business I'll never get to resolve now."

"Oh?"

Janet was quiet for a moment before apparently deciding I was trustworthy. She glanced over to make sure none of the kids were listening in, but they were all busily engaged in their activities. "I auditioned for *The Spirit of '76*. I wanted the Martha Washington role that Rebecca ended up playing." Janet's laugh was short and humorless. "David told me my acting style was outdated and I should stick to teaching kids."

I shook my head. "I'm so sorry. That must have been really hurtful."

"It was." Janet's face turned red with emotion. "I couldn't believe it, to be honest with you. It was totally humiliating. I was a theater major in college. Obviously, I know about acting. But David had to stick his fiancée in the part. Like Rebecca knows anything about drama." She snorted. "And like *David* knew anything about directing or assigning roles. He was telling me that Rebecca 'brought a fresh interpretation to the role.'"

"I'm sorry," I said again.

"And why does Martha Washington need a fresh interpretation?" demanded Janet. "That's like saying Betsy Ross should have been sewing pot holders instead of a flag. I've been working in theater for twenty years. But because I teach high school students, David thought I couldn't handle a serious adult performance." Janet stopped short, fuming.

One of the middle schoolers ran up with a painted backdrop that was still wet. "Ms. McKenzie, where should we put this to dry?"

"Over by the windows, carefully," Janet said. When the child was out of earshot, she continued. "What really bothered me was the way he dismissed my students, too. Like their work wasn't real theater because they're young. The whole thing made me furious."

"It sounds like you had some real differences with David about what constitutes good theater."

"We did," said Janet carefully. "He had very traditional views about who belonged on stage and who didn't. I believe in encouraging fresh voices." She paused before adding, "Though I have to say, he didn't deserve what happened to him."

"You were obviously at the festivities yourself? On the theater float?" I asked.

"No, not on the float—that was just for the kids. I watched them from the crowd, cheering them on. After that, I spent most of the day with my campers, making sure they stayed together and out of trouble."

I said, "Are you usually involved with the Whitby Playhouse? Aside from the July Fourth production?"

"I sure am. I've volunteered there for years and years." Janet pursed her lips. "Lately, things have felt more tense there, though. People seemed on edge even before what happened to David. Rebecca's been acting weird for weeks. Of course, you know David and Rebecca were engaged until a recent breakup."

"I did hear that, yes."

Janet nodded. "Poor Rebecca. In Whitby, gossip spreads like crazy. She's always seemed like she has a lot of pride, and it can't have felt good to have everybody in town talking about you."

"Did you get any inkling what the breakup might have been due to?" I asked.

"Well, Rebecca sure wasn't going to spill anything. She was doing her best to act like nothing had happened. But I could tell she hadn't been sleeping. She probably hadn't been eating, either; she's always been skinny, but she looked like she'd dropped a few pounds."

I said, "Did David say anything? Or did he keep his private life private, too?"

"Yeah, he was pretty private, and who could blame him? Somebody in the theater group did ask him what had happened, and I overheard the answer. All David would say was that he realized he didn't know Rebecca as well as he thought he did." Janet shrugged. "Who knows what that meant. But David's been off for a while, himself. He seemed worried about something besides the production. And maybe besides his breakup with Rebecca."

"Worried how?"

Janet said, "Just distracted. Like his mind was somewhere else entirely. I saw him having what looked like a pretty intense conversation with Pete Brennan. You might know him; he's the insurance guy who handles the theater's finances. Neither one of them looked happy."

Another of the kids called out to Janet, and she gave me a smile. "I'd better go. Good talking to you. The pictures are posting on the paper's social media today?"

"I think so. Keep an eye out for them."

As I walked to the door, Janet called after me. "Ann? I hope they find out what really happened to David. Whatever our differences were, no one should have to go through what his family is dealing with. I feel bad for Angela and her kids."

I nodded and headed back out into the July heat. I walked the short distance to a deli, ordering myself a sandwich to-go. While I was waiting for the order to be ready, I thought about what I'd heard. Janet's resentment toward David was clear, and she'd been on site when David died. But her anger seemed more professional than personal. She felt snubbed, and her feelings were hurt. Was that really enough for her to murder someone?

But then, people had probably killed for less than having their life's work dismissed and their opportunities taken away.

I returned to the library to find what could only be described as controlled chaos. The afternoon crowd was in full swing. There were moms with restless kids on the verge of whininess, teens working on summer assignments (or looking at their phones), and our usual cast of regular patrons settling in for their daily routines.

I'd barely made it through the front door when I heard Zelda's voice, sharper than usual, coming from the general vicinity of the periodicals area.

"Well, if you're going to sit there all day reading every single article, maybe you could at least turn the pages a little more quietly," she was saying, punctuating her words with the aggressive crack of another sunflower seed.

I looked over to see Linus Truman, who followed his library routine religiously, sitting in his usual spot with *The New York Times* held carefully in front of him. He was wearing his customary suit and large spectacles, looking every inch the distinguished gentleman he always appeared to be. His owlish eyes peered over the top of the newspaper at Zelda, who was seated at a nearby table with her smoking cessation books and ever-present bag of sunflower seeds.

"I beg your pardon?" asked Linus in his polite voice.

"The pages," Zelda said, cracking another seed with what seemed like unnecessary force. "You're rustling them like you're trying to start a campfire."

Linus seemed to be genuinely perplexed. "I wasn't aware I was making any noise."

"Well, you are. A lot. Some of us are trying to concentrate." Zelda cracked two more shells, which I felt were certainly louder than Linus turning pages.

I walked over, hoping to defuse the situation before it escalated. Zelda and Linus, although vastly different in personality, were friends. I decided it would behoove me to ensure they stayed that way. "How's everyone doing?"

"Fine," Zelda said curtly. But then she immediately softened when she spotted Owen and Timothy settling down at a computer station nearby. "How's the tech project coming along?" she called out to them.

Owen looked up, beaming. "Great! Timothy's showing me how to update the catalog system."

"Fantastic," said Zelda warmly, before turning back to Linus with considerably less warmth. "Some people around here actually accomplish things with their time."

Linus blinked several times, clearly wondering what transgression he'd committed to deserve Zelda's ire. "But I only come here to read. That's what I'm accomplishing."

"Every day," said Zelda with a snort. "Same schedule, same newspapers and books. Same everything. Don't you want to mix things up?"

"I find routine comforting," Linus replied with dignity. "Especially since my wife passed. But I do mix things up. I'm reading a biography of Theodore Roosevelt this week instead of fiction."

Something in his tone must have penetrated Zelda's nicotine-deprived crankiness, because her expression softened slightly. "Oh. Well, I suppose that does qualify as different."

"My dog Ivy seems to approve of the routine as well," Linus continued, apparently deciding to abandon *The New York Times* for a bit of conversation. "She knows exactly when I'll be home for our afternoon walk. She meets me at the door, her leash in her mouth. Clever animal."

"You have a dog?" Owen asked, looking interested.

Linus's face brightened. "A lovely girl. Large and sweet-natured."

"What kind?" Timothy asked.

"Ah that's information I'm afraid I don't really know. She's a mixed breed of some sort. The veterinarian thinks perhaps some retriever, some shepherd. She has very expressive eyes."

Zelda was looking less ornery by the minute. "Well, I suppose that's nice," she said grudgingly. "Dogs do need a routine. Unlike people, who sometimes need to shake things up." She leveled a pointed look at his newspaper.

"Perhaps," Linus offered diplomatically. "Although I imagine your routine has changed considerably recently. I see you're working hard on quitting smoking."

Zelda's eyes narrowed. "How'd you know that?"

It was fairly obvious, of course. Zelda had a stack of smoking cessation books, a new sunflower eating habit, and a fairly nasty mood.

Linus ignored the question. "How's it going?" he asked instead.

"I'm still not smoking," said Zelda. I could hear the pride in her voice despite her attempt to sound casual. "Though I'll tell you, everyone around here is getting on my last nerve."

"Present company excluded," I said with a smile.

"Naturally," said Zelda as she cracked another sunflower seed.

Linus carefully folded his newspaper and checked his watch. "If you'll excuse me, it's time for me to make my afternoon trip home. Ivy will be expecting her lunch."

Zelda appeared to be looking to fire a parting shot. "How old is that Roosevelt book?" she demanded.

"It was written and published in the seventies," Linus answered.

"Next time, try reading something published this decade."

Linus turned back with what might have been the hint of a smile. "I'll consider it."

After he left, Owen shook his head. "Miss Zelda, you're being kind of cranky today."

"It's because I'm suffering," grated Zelda. "No nicotine. It takes it out of you." She gathered her books and seeds and headed for the circulation desk to check out her books.

Luna appeared at my elbow. "How did the visit with Janet go? Any intel?"

"Sort of. Janet definitely had issues with David. He basically told her she wasn't good enough for community theater."

"Ouch," said Luna.

"Yeah. She also mentioned that David was having some kind of intense conversation with Pete Brennan recently."

Luna frowned. "I feel like I know that name, but I can't place him."

"Pete's an insurance guy. Apparently, he's in charge of the theater finances. But Janet wasn't sure what he and David were talking about."

Luna shook her head. "Sounds like a lot of people had issues with David lately. But poor Jeremy thought David hung the moon." She paused. "Sometimes I think he's super-naïve. Jeremy, I mean, not David."

"He just likes to think the best of people," I said. It was true. And it was actually pretty refreshing to be around someone like that. Maybe opposites attracted more than I thought. Luna wasn't exactly a cynic, but she was fairly pragmatic for someone who dressed like an Earth mother. Luna was also a good deal older than Jeremy.

"Let's talk about something more cheerful," said Luna. "Like your wedding planning. How's it all coming along?"

"It's going okay. Small wedding, you know? Not too much to figure out." I paused. "Well, that's what I keep telling myself, anyway."

But Luna appeared to see right through me. "Hmm. I don't remember that planning a wedding is all rainbows and kittens."

This got my full attention. "You planned a wedding? For yourself?"

"Sure thing. A dress, flowers, venue, the whole shebang." Her voice was as casual as if she were reciting what she'd eaten for breakfast that morning.

"Luna! You never told me you were engaged."

Luna laughed at my expression. "Look at you! You're so very shocked. You didn't realize I had such hidden depths."

"It's a real bombshell. Who was the guy?"

Luna waved her hand dismissively. "Nobody you'd know. Someone in New York, from when I lived there. Anyway, we ended up deciding the wedding stuff was too much hassle. It was too detail-oriented, almost like having a job. It didn't suit our beatnik identities. We decided to elope."

"Wow. I can't believe I'm hearing this story for the first time. That's really romantic."

"Not as romantic as you'd think," said Luna with a grin. "He left me at the altar. Well, not the altar, because it was a court-house. I guess he left me on the courthouse steps. But you know what I mean."

"Ugh. I'm sorry, Luna."

Luna said cheerfully, "Don't be. It's the best thing that ever happened to me, really. I mean, who wants to be hitched to someone who can't handle filling out paperwork at a court-house? Who needs that? And now I get to live vicariously through your wedding planning without any of the stress."

Before I could respond, there was a loud mechanical grind-ing noise from the direction of our long-suffering copy machine, followed by what sounded like someone kicking it.

"Oh, for heaven's sake," came Wilson's voice, sounding un-usually loud and frustrated.

Luna and I hurried over to find Wilson standing in front of the copier, which appeared to be making despondent whirring sounds while blinking an error message. Fitz was sitting nearby, his tail twitching in obvious disapproval of all the mechanical noise. An elderly patron stood by Wilson, looking apologetic.

"Gracious, but I'm sorry. I was just trying to copy my pattern pieces," she said.

Wilson opened the copier and pulled out what appeared to be fabric, along with several pieces of poster board and what looked like glitter. Fitz immediately perked up at the sight of the glitter, his green eyes tracking the sparkly pieces with interest as they drifted to the floor.

"Madam," said Wilson stiffly. "This machine is designed for paper. Regular paper, only. Not fabric, nor poster board, and certainly not materials covered in craft glitter."

Fitz, apparently deciding the situation required his intervention, batted at the escaped glitter with obvious delight. He looked up fetchingly at us, as if trying to relieve the tension he sensed.

"It fit through the slot," said the elderly woman firmly.

"That doesn't mean it should go there," Wilson replied. He held up a piece of fabric that was now decorated with streaks of toner. "This is a copy machine, not a craft press."

Luna was shaking with laughter, which didn't seem to improve Wilson's mood in the slightest. I said, "Maybe we need a sign."

The patron, still a bit on the defensive, agreed. "A sign would be very, very helpful."

"We do have a sign," said Wilson, pointing to a small placard that read 'Paper Only.' Apparently, we need a larger sign. And perhaps a guard."

The patron gathered up her now-ruined craft materials. "I'll just take these to the print shop downtown," she said with a sniff. Her attitude indicated that was a far better option, anyway.

As she walked away, Wilson stared at the copier with the expression of a man seriously considering a career change. Fitz had managed to get glitter stuck on his paws and was now tracking sparkly footprints across the library as he moseyed toward the children's department.

"We'll be finding glitter everywhere for weeks," Wilson muttered, watching Fitz's glittery progress with resignation.

"On the bright side, at least she didn't try to laminate a houseplant in our laminator like that other woman did last month."

Wilson's look suggested he wasn't ready to find any latent humor in the situation yet. "I'm going to call the repair guy. Again."

As he headed to his office, shoulders squared, Luna turned to me with a grin. "And that's why I love working here. There's never a dull moment."

I had to agree. With Zelda's nicotine withdrawal, Wilson's dignified irritation, Luna's surprise romantic history, and the patron's creative interpretation of office equipment, it had certainly been an eventful afternoon.

As I settled back at the reference desk, my mind drifted back to David and Pete Brennan. Whatever they'd been discussing, it sounded serious. I made a mental note to speak with Pete. I also thought it might be useful to speak with my old drama teacher, Carol. Since she was working with the production, she might have some insights into David's dynamics with different people at the theater.

But first, I had to help a patron who was approaching with what appeared to be a very thick craft project folder. "Excuse me," she said hopefully. "Do you think the copier could handle copying my scrapbook pages?"

I glanced toward Wilson's office, where I could hear him on the phone with the repair guy. I looked back at the woman's folder, which appeared to contain materials that were definitely not standard paper.

"Let me refer you to the print shop. It's right down the street. They're much better equipped for special projects."

Chapter Nine

That evening, I filled Grayson in on my visit with Janet over a takeout Margherita pizza at my house. He was especially interested in what she'd said about David and Pete's talk.

"Maybe David was trying to advise Pete on the theater finances," said Grayson. "David seems like the kind of guy who wasn't opposed to giving unwanted advice."

"Or maybe the two of them just didn't get along, period. Then they're working together on the play and it ended up being too much time together."

"Worth looking into," Grayson said, nodding thoughtfully. "What's your next step?"

"I was thinking that I should talk with Carol Winters. She always seems really observant and on top of things. She may have good information on what was going on behind the scenes at the production. Maybe she knows more about why David and Pete weren't getting along. With that information, I could get farther with talking to Pete after that."

"Good plan. Carol strikes me as someone who doesn't miss much."

We spent the rest of the evening talking about wedding plans and pretending we weren't both thinking about murder. It felt like a minor victory.

At the library the next morning, I was updating the summer reading program display when I spotted Carol Winters at one of our computer stations. Considering that I'd been planning how to speak with her without seeming nosy, this was a real stroke of luck. But after all, she was a fairly regular patron. She checked out the odd book, but mainly wanted time on the computer. I'd gathered in the past that she didn't have a computer at home.

Carol was leaning forward, staring intently at the computer screen with the sort of forced concentration I usually associated with people doing important research. She had a satisfied smile on her face, like someone who'd just solved a puzzle. She was taking notes in a small notebook and occasionally glancing around as if making sure no one was peering over her shoulder.

I finished arranging the display books and casually walked over. "Ms. Winters? How are you doing?"

She looked up, momentarily startled, then quickly minimized whatever she'd been looking at on the screen. "Oh! Hello Ann. I've told you before to call me Carol. I'm not your teacher anymore, you know."

"Thanks, Carol." It still felt weird using her first name, regardless of the fact that I was now in my early-thirties and not my teens anymore.

"I still remember when you played the narrator in our spring production of 'Our Town.' You had such a lovely speaking voice."

I smiled at her. "That's nice of you to say so and kind of you to remember. It feels like a million years ago now. I remember I was super-nervous on opening night."

Carol said, "Well, it didn't show. And, you might be surprised, but nerves can actually be good for theater. It means you care about doing a good job." Her expression grew wistful. "I loved those productions. Seeing young people discover their voices and gain confidence was a wonderful thing. There's nothing quite like watching a shy teenager bloom on stage."

"You were a terrific teacher," I said, meaning it. "I know lots of students who still talk about your classes."

"That's sweet of you to say. I do still miss it, you know. I loved the energy and creativity of it all. But these days I have to get my theater fix volunteering with the community productions."

I said, "The Fourth of July play was excellent. I really enjoyed it."

Carol said, "Well, it was as good as it could be under the circumstances. Poor Rebecca was quite rattled by David's death, of course. She had a tough time remembering her lines, but who wouldn't? It was so odd not to have David there when he'd been directing us since the beginning of the production."

"I'm sure it was. What was David like as a director?"

Carol said, "Oh, he was quite capable. He was a very organized person, you see. Most thorough. I will say he had his own way of doing things that might have differed from how I'd have approached it, but his way seemed equally effective."

"Did you have any concerns about his methods?"

Carol considered this. "I wouldn't say I had *concerns*. But he was quite decisive. David knew what he wanted and wasn't particularly interested in suggestions from others. That's often how directors work, of course. They don't rule by committee."

"It must have been frustrating, though, for someone with your experience," I guessed.

"Perhaps a little. But I understood my role was to support, not lead. Of course, I couldn't help myself when it came to jotting down notes about everything, including David's directorial style. That's how I keep from opening my mouth and trying to take over." Carol gave a rueful smile.

"That's smart. I'm sure it would feel natural to try and step in and direct yourself." I paused. "I'm sorry about David. I know that must have been so hard for everyone involved in the production. And the show still went ahead, even though it was a tough day for you all."

"A tough day indeed, my dear. I was at the festivities all day. I watched the parade, took a few photos, and cheered on the floats. I really can't resist a parade. I thought the high school marching band did a marvelous job. Then after the parade, I helped set up for the performance."

I said, "Did you see David on the Fourth?"

Carol's expression grew more serious. "I did, actually. He seemed quite preoccupied with something that morning. I believe it must have been more than just being nervous about the play later that day. He kept checking his watch and looking around as if he was expecting someone."

"Did you speak with David? Or get a sense of what he might have been worried about?"

Carol shook her head regretfully. "I'm not sure what it was, I'm afraid. Nor did I speak with him. But I did notice he seemed particularly interested in speaking with *certain* people. He also appeared to have a rather vehement conversation with someone."

"Oh?"

Carol hesitated, then said carefully, "Well I do try not to eavesdrop, however I did observe him speaking with Rebecca on the morning of the Fourth. Do you know her? She and David had been engaged to be married."

"Yes, that's what I heard."

Carol continued, "They seemed to be having a personal discussion. I couldn't hear most of it, but it seemed she was trying to convince David of something. Rebecca appeared quite upset and David seemed most uncomfortable." Carol lowered her voice. "I did catch him saying something. I didn't know what he meant, though. He said 'you know why I needed to break off the engagement.' But then they moved farther away, and they were no longer within earshot." Carol's face reflected her disappointment. Clearly, she had been interested in their little tête-à-tête.

"I'm sure the broken engagement was difficult for both of them."

"I'd imagine so," Carol said. "Rebecca has been rather emotional lately about their relationship. I think she hoped they might reconcile, but David seemed quite firm about moving on."

"Did you notice David being at odds with anyone else lately?" I asked. "I'm just trying to understand what might have been troubling him."

Carol nodded thoughtfully. "Now that you mention it, yes. He seemed unhappy with Pete Brennan. Pete handles the treasurer duties for our theater group. They did seem to be having an intense discussion recently."

"Intense how?"

"Well, David looked rather serious, and Pete seemed to be explaining something at great length. Pete was gesturing with his hands the way he does when he's gotten himself worked up." Carol paused, considering. "I couldn't hear what they were saying, but David didn't look particularly pleased with whatever Pete was telling him."

I waited, hoping she'd elaborate.

"Actually," Carol continued, "I remember David mentioning Pete to me a few weeks ago during one of our rehearsals. Nothing specific, mind you, but he said something like 'I'm not crazy about how Pete handles things.' I got the impression David might have had some concerns about Pete's work with the theater, though he didn't go into details."

"Did David say what kind of concerns?"

Carol shook her head. "No, he was quite private about it. But you know how David was—very methodical and organized. I think he might have found Pete's more casual and flippant approach to work a bit frustrating."

Then Carol looked over at the computer and said wryly, "Goodness. I appear to be quite the gossip. Perhaps I should quit while I'm ahead and get back to my research. Although perhaps I've already gotten what I need." She looked pleased by this and perhaps just a little smug.

"Can I help you with anything?"

"Oh no, I don't think so. I'm just keeping track of various community matters. You'd be surprised how much information is available if you know where to look. I do believe in being thorough."

Before I could ask more, Timothy approached our table. As usual, he was accruing volunteer hours at the library for his college applications. "Mrs. Winters? I'm sorry to interrupt, but your computer time is about to expire. Would you like to extend it?"

"That's all right, dear. I believe I have everything I need now." She gathered her notebook and purse. "Ann, it was lovely speaking with you. It's always such a pleasure to talk with my former students."

She stood to leave, then paused. "You know, teaching was the most rewarding thing I ever did. I never married, but I feel like I have all these children whom I watched grow up. Such an honor. And now, I'm still enjoying being involved with the Whitby Theater. Maybe it helps keep me feeling connected with something I care about."

There was something almost lonely in her voice, and I felt a pang of sympathy for her. I remembered her passion as a drama teacher, how present she seemed in the classroom, and her genuine enjoyment of her students. I gave her a hug, telling her how I felt. She hugged me back and there was a lift in her step as she left the library.

Chapter Ten

Later, I was at the reference desk when my phone buzzed with a text from Grayson. *Want to grab lunch and visit Pete Brennan? He's one of the newspaper's advertisers, and I thought I'd do a community spotlight piece. I could use the company.*

I glanced at the clock. It was nearly noon, and after my conversation with Carol, I was curious to hear what Pete might have to say about David and the theater group. I texted Grayson back to let him know I'd meet him at Pete's office in ten minutes.

The insurance company was in a small brick building on Main Street, wedged between the hardware store and an accounting firm. It was just a short walk from the library. The window displayed faded posters advertising car and home insurance, and a hand-lettered sign that read "Brennan Insurance—Three Generations of Service."

Grayson was waiting outside when I walked up. "Thanks for coming along," he said, giving me a quick kiss on the cheek. "Pete's been advertising with us for years, and I thought it would be nice to feature one of our longtime supporters."

"And ask him about murder?" I asked, quirking a brow.

Grayson grinned at me. "That too. I might let you lead that part."

The office was small and cluttered, with metal filing cabinets lining one wall and a reception area that looked like it hadn't been updated since the 1980s. The door had a bell that rang when we walked in, and Pete Brennan emerged from a back office. He was in his early fifties, wearing a conservative suit that was perhaps just a bit worn at the edges. He had thinning hair, and the slightly harried look of someone trying to juggle too many responsibilities.

"Grayson!" Pete's face lit up with a smile that seemed genuine. "What brings you by? Please tell me you're not here to raise my advertising rates."

Grayson laughed. "Nothing like that. I'm actually working on a series about local businesses that support the community. I thought you might be interested in being featured."

Pete now looked pleasantly surprised. "Really? Sure, that would be awesome. Please, have a seat." He gestured to two chairs across from his desk. "And this is . . . ?"

"Ann Beckett," I said, reaching over to shake his hand. "I hope you don't mind me tagging along."

Pete shook my hand, then smiled. "Of course. I remember you from the library. It's hard for me to place people when I see them in a different place. Wait a minute. You're Grayson's fiancée, aren't you? The one making his grin extra-large every day. Nice to meet you. And if the two of you ever want to think about life insurance, give me a holler. I could give you friend rates."

"We'll do that," I said with a return smile.

Grayson pulled out his phone to record. "Just tell me about your business, your involvement with the community, that sort of thing."

Pete straightened in his chair, clearly pleased to be the center of attention. "Well, as the sign says, this is a three-generation business. My grandfather started Brennan Insurance back in 1952, my dad took over in the 70s, and I've been running things for the past fifteen years."

"That's quite a lot of legacy," I said. "It must be a lot of responsibility carrying that on."

"It is," Pete agreed, his composure slipping slightly for a moment. "Especially these days. The insurance business isn't what it used to be. There's all this competition from the big companies, people shopping online, and stuff like that." He caught himself. "But we're the business who has deep roots in the community, and that's what matters."

Grayson said, "Speaking of community involvement, I understand you volunteer for the theater group."

Pete's expression grew more somber. "That's right. I've handled the community theater's financial affairs for the past several years. That's their bookkeeping, insurance, and whatnot. The theater group also helps with setup, takedown, and decorating for town events. It's sort of a way for us to give back to Whitby and also raise awareness of the theater."

I said in a gentle tone, "I'm sorry about David. That must have been really hard."

Pete's face fell. "It was tough. David was a good guy. He was super-organized and really detail-oriented. He always cared about doing things right, you know?" He shook his head. "I still can't believe somebody did that to him. He was in the prime of his life."

"Did you know David well?" asked Grayson.

"Pretty well. David wasn't just the director of the play, he was also involved in helping run the theater. We had monthly meetings, budget reviews, and that kind of thing. He always wanted to make sure we were running a tight ship. He liked dotting every I and crossing every t. Sometimes I think he worried a little too much about details. There were only so many hours in the day, and our theater involvement wasn't our full-time job."

We had definitely strayed off our stated reason for the visit, but Pete didn't seem to notice. He looked as if he'd been punched in the gut at the mention of David.

"Did David work well with the others at the theater?" I asked.

"Well, you know how it goes. When we got closer to opening night, there was more tension. David was definitely tense, too. People seemed on edge even before what happened to David."

Grayson tilted his head curiously. "Was there more tension than usual?"

"Well, I shouldn't gossip, but Rebecca had been acting pretty strange. She seemed distracted and almost removed. Then there was Angela—she was David's sister. Apparently, she's been under a bunch of financial pressure after her divorce. David was fussing at her about her spending habits."

I asked, "Was she spending more than she should?"

Pete shrugged. "I don't know. David seemed to think she was. Oh, I shouldn't say that. I don't know what David was really thinking. But he did say he thought she was making some questionable financial decisions. He asked me a few times whether I thought she was handling her finances responsibly." Pete looked uncomfortable. "I probably shouldn't have said anything about that. It's not really my business."

"Was David worried about anything else?"

Pete considered this. "He was just about as distracted as Rebecca was. I guess that was understandable, given their broken engagement. Had you heard about that?" When Grayson and I nodded, Pete said, "Yeah, he was probably mostly moody because of their relationship imploding. But there was more than just that."

"It must have been such a shock when you heard about David," I said. "Were you still helping with the volunteering when you heard about it?"

"Yeah, I was there all day, volunteering, and that's when I got the news about David. Just awful. I felt like I was in a daze, kind of going through the motions after hearing about him." Pete managed a small smile. "David and I were supposed to meet that afternoon to go over final expense reports, but it never happened."

Pete's voice grew heavy as he continued. "David was one of the good ones, you know? He was always trying to do right by everybody. I keep thinking that if maybe he minded his own business a little more, this might never have happened."

"What do you mean?" Grayson asked.

Pete looked as if he'd said more than he intended. "Nothing specific. Just that David had a tendency to insert himself in the middle of other people's problems. Sometimes that creates all kinds of unforeseen complications."

Pete glanced up at a wall clock. "I should probably get back to it," he said, sounding reluctant. "But before I do, did you need anything else for your article?"

He seemed eager to shift back to safer ground, unwilling to throw any suspicion at anyone.

Grayson said, "Let's talk a little about the services you offer and your approach to customer service."

Twenty minutes later, Grayson had gotten everything he needed for the article. As we prepared to leave, Pete stood and walked us to the door. "I hope they find whoever did this," he said, his concern sounding genuine. "David deserved so much better than what happened to him."

Outside, Grayson and I walked in silence for a few moments in the parking lot. He finally said, "What do you think?"

I considered this. "He seemed genuinely upset about David. It sounds like they spent a good deal of time together. I felt like he was holding information back, though."

Grayson nodded. "I got the same feeling. You think he might have had something to hide?"

"I'm not sure. It's either that, or he just didn't want to talk about the people who might have had a motive to kill David. He sounded like he felt bad about gossiping, even though he gave us information. Maybe he didn't want to throw anybody under the bus."

"Right," Grayson said. He sighed. "Well, hopefully Pete doesn't know too much. People who *do* have information about a crime rarely seem to live very long." He paused, looking at me with concern. "Hey, we need to get you some lunch before your break is over."

"No, it's okay. I packed a lunch today. I'll just eat really fast before I head back to the reference desk."

Grayson gave me a lift to the library. Although the building was nearby, the July humidity had come out in full force.

The next morning at the library, I arrived to find Wilson pacing in his office, looking more agitated than usual. Through his glass windows, I could see him checking his watch repeatedly and adjusting his tie.

"What's going on with Wilson?" I asked Luna as she walked up to me.

"No idea, but he's been like that since he got here. Maybe the library board called another emergency meeting?"

Timothy walked in for his volunteer shift, followed by Zelda with Owen in tow. I was relieved to see Zelda appeared significantly less irritable than she had been.

"Still no cigarettes," she announced to no one in particular as she crunched a sunflower seed. "And my cravings are going away a little."

"You're doing great," said Timothy, grinning at her. Owen looked proudly at the older woman.

Wilson emerged from his office, still looking flustered. He was patting his suit jacket pocket distractedly.

"Staff meeting," he announced abruptly. "Conference room. Now."

Luna and I exchanged glances. Wilson's staff meetings were usually scheduled well in advance and came with agendas. This felt more like panic.

We all gathered in the small conference room, even Timothy, Zelda, and Owen, who had apparently been swept along by the force of Wilson's urgency. Wilson stood at the head of the table, still patting at his pocket absently. His tie was slightly crooked, and there was a thin sheen of perspiration on his forehead. He didn't seem to notice that it wasn't just Luna and me in the room.

Luna whispered in my ear. "Is he having a minor stroke?"

"I've called this meeting to address something." Wilson cleared his throat. "The library board called an emergency meeting earlier about implementing new safety protocols after the tragic death at the parade. They're also requiring immediate documentation of all current expenditures for an audit review."

Wilson again absently patted his pocket before just as absently reaching into it to pull out the offending item. It was a velvet box. He peered at it as if he'd never seen it before, before quickly attempting to shove it into his pants pocket.

Unfortunately, his pocket was already occupied by his keys, and the box bounced off, landing on the floor.

The small velvet cube bounded under the conference table, and our ever-helpful Timothy dropped to his hands and knees to retrieve it.

"You dropped this," Timothy said, popping back up and offering the box.

Wilson's face turned an alarming shade of scarlet. "That's not . . . I mean, it's just . . ."

Owen, with the directness that the very young possess, asked, "Is that an engagement ring?"

The silence in the room was deafening. Wilson looked as if he wanted to sink into the floor. Luna's mouth had dropped open, and even Zelda had stopped her infernal crunching of sunflower seeds.

"Wilson," said Luna slowly, "are you planning on proposing to my mom?"

Wilson adjusted the tie. However, it was just as askew as it had been before his adjustment. "Well. You see . . . " But he couldn't seem to summon the next words. I'd never seen him so very incoherent.

At that exact moment, as if summoned by some cosmic sense of terrible timing, Mona appeared in the doorway. She was carrying what appeared to be homemade muffins and wearing a cheerful yellow dress.

"Hello everyone! I thought I'd bring some blueberry muffins in. You're having a staff meeting? I thought those were a different day of the week." She stopped short, taking in the scene. Wilson was red-faced and flustered, Timothy was still holding a ring box, and everyone else frozen in silence.

"Oh my," Mona said softly.

Wilson, apparently deciding that if he was going to be mortified, he might as well be mortified thoroughly, took the ring box from Timothy and turned toward Mona. He cleared his throat. "Mona. I've considered the matter and believe our relationship has progressed to a point where I believe it would be appropriate for further steps."

His formal tone sounded much the same as the one he used for board presentations. "I would like to request your consideration of a matrimonial arrangement."

Luna buried her face in her hands, stifling what sounded like a peal of laughter. I hid a smile. Wilson had apparently forgotten the proposal he and I had practiced.

Mona, however, was beaming. She set down the muffins on the conference table and walked over to Wilson, who was still standing stiffly with the ring box sitting on his outstretched hand.

"Wilson," she said gently, "are you asking me to marry you?"

"Yes," Wilson said, relief evident in his voice. "Yes, as a matter of fact, I am."

"Then I accept. With joy."

Wilson's formal posture collapsed as if someone had cut his strings. "Really? You do? You . . . yes?"

"I do, yes. Of *course*, you silly man." Mona stood on her tiptoes and kissed his cheek, which made him turn an even deeper shade of red.

Owen started clapping, and we all joined in. Then everyone started speaking at once.

Luna jumped up from her chair. "This is incredible!" She hugged them both, practically bouncing with excitement. "I can't believe you didn't tell me you were planning this, Wilson."

"Can we see the ring?" Timothy asked.

"Wilson, you sly devil," Zelda said with approval. "Though next time rehearse that speech. You sounded like you were reading the tax code."

Owen, focused on the practical matters, asked, "Does this mean we can have the wedding cake at the library?"

The chaos was interrupted by the arrival of my favorite patron, Linus Truman, who appeared in the doorway in his customary suit. He was gingerly holding what appeared to be a child's art project covered in sequins and glitter.

"I beg your pardon," he said politely. "Someone left his by the copy machine. I thought it best to turn it in before the sequins ended up everywhere. Or before they put it inside the paper tray."

Wilson winced at the mention of more craft supplies near his library equipment.

"He got engaged!" Owen announced helpfully.

Linus's owlish eyes brightened as he carefully set down the sparkly artwork. "Congratulations are in order, then. That's marvelous news."

It took another ten minutes for everyone to calm down enough for Wilson to dismiss his impromptu staff meeting. Then he and Mona, looking rather shy but happy, headed out the door for a celebratory meal.

It was hard to get back to work after the excitement of the proposal. Everyone else was chatting with each other. Luna was bouncing around and being far too loud in the children's section. I was just getting settled at the reference desk when my phone rang. It was Jeremy.

"Are you busy?" he asked. "Ready to run our errand with Luna?"

I had absolutely no idea what Jeremy was referring to. But if it involved Luna, this was completely understandable. "Which errand is that?"

"Hoo-boy. Sounds like she forgot to mention it to you. We need to return the stuff from the library's July Fourth display back to the Whitby Playhouse. Luna said there are some heavy pieces, and I thought I could help carry them."

I said, "That sounds great. It's very quiet at the library now, so it's probably a good time to go."

Jeremy arrived fifteen minutes later. He picked up Luna and me, along with several boxes of period costumes and props that had been part of our historical display. Luna quickly filled Jeremy in on the engagement news.

"I still can't believe Wilson proposed during a staff meeting," Luna said as we headed for the theater. "Although it was absolutely perfect in the most awkward way possible. Very Wilson."

"And it worked," Jeremy pointed out. "Your mom said yes."

"She'd have said yes if he'd proposed in the grocery store parking lot," said Luna fondly. "She's been crazy about him for months."

We drove the short distance to the Whitby Playhouse. A couple of minutes later, we knocked on a side door, but no one answered. Luna tried opening the door, which was unlocked. The building was quiet and dim, with that particular smell of dust, old wood, and decades of performances that old theaters have.

"Carol told me she'd meet us here to show us where everything goes," Luna said, glancing around. "She's been trying to organize all the storage areas here."

"Carol?" I called out. "We're here with the library display stuff."

There was no answer. We stood in the hallway for a moment, listening.

"Maybe she's in the storage room," Jeremy suggested.

We made our way down a narrow hallway behind the stage, carrying the boxes. The storage room door was open.

"Carol?" Luna called as we approached the doorway.

The storage room was larger than I'd expected, filled with costume racks, prop boxes, and shelves lined with programs, photographs, and other theater memorabilia dating back years.

"Wow," I said, looking around. "There's a lot of history in here."

Luna said, "Yeah, Carol's been working hard to organize this stuff—" Her voice cut off abruptly. She was looking toward the far corner of the room, her face pale.

"Luna?" Jeremy asked. "What's wrong?"

I followed Luna's gaze and felt my stomach drop.

Carol Winters was lying on the floor behind one of the costume racks. She wasn't moving, and there was a length of rope—the kind used for rigging curtains—around her neck.

Chapter Eleven

"No," breathed Jeremy.

I hurried to Carol, feeling for a pulse. Finding none, I fumbled for my phone, my hands shaking as I called 911. Luna sank into a nearby chair, staring at Carol's still form.

"This is Ann Beckett," I said in a shaky voice when the dispatcher answered. "We need police and an ambulance at the Whitby Playhouse. We've found a body."

As I gave the dispatcher the address, I looked around the storage room. Carol's notebook was lying open on a nearby table, filled with her characteristic detailed notes. There were papers scattered on the floor, and some boxes looked askew, as if they'd been disturbed during a struggle.

"The police are on their way," I told Luna and Jeremy. "We should wait for them outside the building."

After we stepped outside, Luna teared up. "Carol was so excited about getting that room organized. She'd been working on it for weeks."

Jeremy put an arm around her shoulders. "I know. She didn't deserve this."

Within minutes, we heard sirens outside. Burton arrived first, followed by what looked like the entire state police force. They quickly established a crime scene, briefly took our statements, and asked us to wait for any further questions.

Burton emerged from the theater building twenty minutes later, looking grim. The state police had taken over the scene inside, and I could see through the windows that there were crime scene technicians moving around. The same yellow tape that surrounded the gazebo on the Fourth now cordoned off the entrance.

"I need to speak with each of you separately," Burton said, his voice gentle but official. "Ann, could I start with you?"

He led me to his patrol car, where we sat in the front seats with the doors open to catch what little breeze there was in the humid July air. Burton pulled out his familiar notebook and pencil stub.

"Could you walk me through finding Carol?" he asked. "From the beginning."

I took a deep breath, trying to organize my thoughts. "Jeremy called me about returning the library display case items to the theater. He picked up Luna and me. Luna was supposed to meet Carol so she could show us where everything went."

"What time was this arranged?"

"I'm not sure when Luna and Carol originally set it up. Jeremy called me about an hour ago." I paused, thinking. "Luna said Carol had been working on organizing the storage area of the Whitby Playhouse for a while."

Burton jotted down notes. "When you arrived, was the theater locked?"

"We knocked first, but no one answered. Luna tried the side door, and it was unlocked. We called out for Carol as soon as we walked inside."

"Did you notice anything unusual? Any sounds or signs of disturbance?"

I shook my head. "The building was quiet. I didn't hear anything." I felt a bit of frisson shooting up my spine at the thought that Carol's killer could have been hiding in the building, perhaps leaving after we walked further in. I took a deep breath and said, "We went straight to the storage room because that's where Luna expected to find Carol." I cleared my throat. "She was just lying there behind the costume rack."

Burton waited while I thought for a few moments. "It did seem to me like maybe the boxes in the storage area had been bumped around. The room looked so organized that the boxes stood out a little. Maybe the murderer accidentally bumped them when he heard us come in?" My voice caught slightly on the words.

Burton's expression softened. "I know this is tough. You've had a hard week."

"This is connected to David's murder, isn't it? Surely, it has to be."

He didn't answer directly. "What can you tell me about Carol? Has she been acting any differently lately? Have you noticed any changes?"

I thought about the conversation we'd had at work. "I didn't know Carol super well. She'd taught me drama when I was in high school. But I did just see her at the library. Actually, she was acting a little secretive. Or maybe that's the wrong word. She was definitely trying to maintain privacy, which is something we value at the library, of course."

Burton's pencil stopped moving. "Secretive or private how, exactly?"

"Carol kept glancing around while she was working, like she was making sure no one was watching. She said she was doing research on something related to the community." I paused. "She seemed to have that satisfied look people get when they've solved a puzzle."

Burton asked, "Did she tell you anything else during your conversation?"

"Carol mentioned seeing David having some intense talks with both Rebecca and Pete Brennan. She said David seemed preoccupied with something other than just opening night nerves."

Burton carefully made a few notes. "Anything else you recall?"

"She said Rebecca had been acting strange for weeks, even before her engagement with David ended. Carol said she overheard David telling Rebecca 'You know why I needed to break off the engagement.'"

Burton's pencil stopped moving again. "He said that?"

"That's what she told me. She said she didn't know what it meant." I took in Burton's concerned expression. "Do you think Carol discovered something dangerous?"

"I think," Burton said carefully, "that Carol was the kind of person who paid attention. She liked to know what was going on around town. She probably even documented it. And sometimes those types of traits can put someone in danger."

A state police detective approached the car. "Chief? We need you inside for a few minutes."

"I have a couple more quick interviews, then I'll be right there." Burton got out of the car as the detective headed back to the theater. "Why don't you take the rest of the day off, Ann? Take tomorrow off too, if you need it. Luna should, too."

"Well, we're supposed to be working."

Burton shook his head. "Wilson will understand. I'll call him myself." Burton's tone was firm but kind. "You're been through enough. And Ann? Be careful. Until we figure out what's going on, I want you to stay alert. Don't go anywhere alone if you can help it."

The seriousness in his voice sent a chill through me despite the summer heat.

After Burton spoke with Luna and Jeremy, we headed back to the library in a subdued silence. Luna sat in the passenger seat, occasionally wiping tears from her eyes.

"I just can't believe Carol's gone," Luna said somberly as Jeremy pulled into the library parking lot. "She was so *alive*, you know? So vital."

Jeremy parked the car. "This is really scary, you guys. Two murders in four days? In Whitby?"

It had happened before, but that didn't make the situation any better.

Luna said, "And whoever did this is still out there." She looked smaller and more vulnerable than I'd ever seen her.

Wilson, who'd apparently been briefed by Burton, met us at the library entrance, his face creased with worry. The happy glow from his morning engagement seemed to have dimmed considerably.

"I heard what happened," he said. "Are you all right?"

"We're okay," I said, although I wasn't entirely sure how true that was. "Burton told us to take the rest of the day off." I was still trying to shrug off the suggestion, but now it somehow felt harder to do. My mind was buzzing with thoughts about what had happened, and I felt like I needed some time to sort it all out.

"Of course. Take tomorrow off, too."

This was so very unlike Wilson that I did a double-take to make sure I was speaking to the right person.

Seeing me study him, Wilson said, "Nothing is more important than your health. Besides, it's been very quiet at the library. Most people are still probably out of town following the July Fourth holiday. After Burton contacted me to let me know what happened, I made a couple of calls and brought in some more staff."

Luna said, "You're probably not going to believe this Wilson, but I believe I might just work today and tomorrow. Staying busy is probably good for me right now."

Wilson looked like he wanted to argue, but seemed to understand. "Very well. But you're welcome to change your mind at any time." He looked questioningly at me, and I said, "I might go home, actually. But I need to collect my things, and Fitz, of course."

As we walked into the library, I could tell that word of Carol's death had already started spreading. As Wilson had stated, there weren't a lot of patrons in the building. But those who were there were speaking in hushed tones, and there was a tension in the air that hadn't been there earlier.

Zelda was at her usual table with Owen, but instead of her smoking cessation books, she had what appeared to be a stack of security pamphlets. She looked up as I approached.

"I heard about Carol Winters," she said grimly, crunching a sunflower seed with unusual force. "The stress might make me start up smoking again."

"That's not a good idea, Miss Zelda," said Owen, his face worried.

"You're right, kid." She patted his shoulder, a gesture intended to be sweet, but was likely rougher than she thought. "I can't let a murderer mess up my quit streak." Zelda fixed me with a stern look. "Are you carrying pepper spray?"

"I, well, no."

"You should be. Two murders in four days means somebody in this town has lost use of their mind." She gestured to her security pamphlets. "I'm looking into alarm systems. Maybe some motion-sensor lights, too." Zelda's eyes narrowed. "And I'll put a baseball bat next to my bed."

I began to feel very sorry for anyone breaking into Zelda's house.

Chapter Twelve

I should have realized that making it out of the library was going to take longer than I'd planned . One of our regular patrons came up to chat with me for a few minutes. She seemed not to notice how very distracted I was. Finally, she went on her way, but before I slipped out, the library doors opened and Pete Brennan walked in. He looked haggard, with his usual neat appearance somewhat disheveled. He scanned the library, then started walking toward me. I walked away from Zelda and Owen to speak to Pete privately.

"I heard about Carol," he said, his voice hoarse. "And you found her? That's another body you found?"

I told myself that Pete wasn't throwing accusations around, but it somehow seemed that way. I nodded. "I was with a group of other people this time."

"I can't believe it," he continued, almost as if he hadn't heard me. "First David, now Carol. What's happening?"

"I'm sorry," I said. "You must have been close to Carol, since you were both so heavily involved in theater."

Pete nodded absently. "Who'd want to hurt her? She was just a retired teacher."

"It's terrible," I agreed, watching Pete's face carefully. He seemed genuinely distressed.

"The police just finished with me at the office," he went on, still looking rattled. "They came by, asking me a bunch of questions about my whereabouts and the last time I saw Carol. It's like they think everybody in the theater group is a suspect." He laughed, but it came out shaky and hollow. "I know they have to investigate, but it feels surreal."

Zelda, who couldn't seem to refrain from general meddling, sauntered up. She surveyed Pete with her sharp eyes. "Where were you today?"

Pete looked startled, taking a step back. "Excuse me?"

"You heard me. I think it's time for people involved with the Whitby Playhouse to start offering up alibis, don't you?"

Pete frowned. "I was at my office, working on client files."

Zelda gave a languid shrug of a thin shoulder. "Okay. Although that's not much of an alibi. You see, it sure sounds to me like whoever's doing this knew Carol's schedule pretty well."

An uncomfortable silence settled over us. Pete shifted his weight from foot to foot, clearly ill at ease. But then, Zelda's manner would make anyone uneasy.

"Well," Pete said finally. "I should let you all get back to work." He started away but then turned. "I did want to see if any of you knew about a memorial service for David. Have you heard anything?"

"I haven't heard of any arrangements being made yet," I said.

After he left, Zelda leaned over to me. "That man's as nervous as a long-tailed cat in a room full of rocking chairs."

"He's probably just upset about Carol," I said, but I'd noticed Pete's agitation, too.

"Maybe," said Zelda skeptically. "Or maybe he knows something he's not telling."

Then Zelda, usually a fan of people keeping their noses to the grindstone and working hard, gave me a hard look. "You should go home. Get some rest. You look kind of peaked."

If Zelda was telling me to go, I must really not be at my personal best. "Okay. I'll head out." I looked around for Fitz, who I spotted near the children's section, apparently conducting his own investigation on whether any of the glitter from the morning's copier incident had been overlooked. "Come on Fitz. Let's go home."

Fitz looked up at me with those intelligent green eyes, as if sensing something was off. He trotted over immediately, brushing up against me with concern.

A few minutes later, when I'd reached my cottage, I was relieved to be back.

Fitz made a beeline for his water bowl in the kitchen, then returned to wind around my ankles. He gave an inquisitive meow, the one that always sounded like a question.

"It's been quite a day, buddy," I said, reaching down and gently scratching behind his ears. "Carol's gone. Someone killed her, just like David."

Fitz sat back on his haunches and studied my face with that uncanny way cats have of seeming to understand exactly what you're saying. Then he padded over to his favorite spot on the windowsill and settled in to keep watch over the front yard.

I was just relaxing in one of my overstuffed gingham chairs when I heard a car in the driveway. Through the window, I could see Grayson's familiar figure heading toward the house, moving quicker than usual.

Fitz chirped a meow from his perch, having spotted Grayson as well.

A moment later, there was a quick knock at the door before Grayson let himself in with his key. His face was creased with concern, and he crossed the room in three quick strides to pull me into his arms.

"Are you okay?" he asked, his voice muffled against my hair. "I came as soon as I heard. Burton gave me a heads-up."

"I'm all right," I said, leaning into his embrace. "Just tired. It's been a long day."

"I hate that you found another body."

"I wasn't alone this time," I said. "Luna and Jeremy were with me."

"That doesn't make it any less awful." Grayson settled into the chair across from me, but he was perched on the edge like he was ready to spring into action if needed. "Tell me what happened."

I walked him through finding Carol in the theater storage room, Burton's questions, and the aftermath at the library.

"David's and Carol's deaths have got to be connected," Grayson said finally. "Right?"

"They have to be. Two people involved in the same theater production, murdered days apart? That's not a coincidence." I rubbed my temples, feeling a headache starting up. "Carol was researching something at the library, Grayson. She was being secretive about it, but she looked satisfied, as if she'd solved some sort of puzzle."

"What kind of research was it?" asked Grayson.

"I don't know. She said it was something to do with the community, but she didn't want to go into details. She minimized her computer screen when I walked up to her."

Grayson was quiet for a moment. "I wonder what she'd found out. And whether it had something to do with her murder." He sighed, rubbing his forehead absently. "Unfortunately, I should get back to the office to work on the story for tomorrow. Are you sure you're okay?"

"I'll be fine. I'm going to turn in early with Fitz. And Zelda's probably watching the street from her window anyway. Nothing's going to get past her."

We shared a chuckle at that. Fitz, hearing his name, hopped down from the windowsill and belatedly claimed Grayson's lap, purring loudly.

"At least someone's having a good day," Grayson said, gently stroking Fitz's fur. "What's your plan for tomorrow?"

"Well, I'm not working. Burton and Wilson put the kibosh on that."

Grayson frowned. "Oh, hey, before I forget, David's memorial service is tomorrow afternoon. Angela called the paper this morning to place a last-minute obituary."

"Got it. I'm sure Angela's probably trying to get the service behind her. I can't blame her. She's probably looking for a little closure for herself and her kids." I looked at Grayson's worried face. "It's okay. You can head on out. I know you need to work on the article. Like you said, it's going to be a big story."

"It can wait an hour." Grayson settled back in his chair, careful not to disturb Fitz. "Right now, I just want to make sure you're really okay."

And for the first time since finding Carol's body, I felt like maybe I actually was.

Chapter Thirteen

The memorial service for David Hollister was held at a historic church downtown with ivy trailing over its brick façade. Despite the short notice, the pews were full with a mix of Whitby Playhouse members and other Whitby residents who'd known David during his three years in town.

Angela stood at the pulpit to give her eulogy, composed but visibly struggling, her hands trembling as she read from her printed remarks. Her teenage children sat in the front row. Tyler was slumped with his arms crossed, Emma sitting straight-backed.

"David believed in community," Angela said, her voice steady but strained. "He was here to be closer to family, and he threw himself into making Whitby his home. Whether it was directing the July Fourth play or just helping a neighbor, David always wanted to make things better." She gave a short laugh. "Sometimes he cared so much it could be overwhelming, actually. But that was just David. He loved deeply and wanted to protect all the people he cared about."

Jeremy spoke next, sharing memories of David as a colleague who'd always brought fresh perspectives to their team meetings.

"David was the guy who'd remember your birthday or ask about your plans for the weekend. He made work feel less like work." Luna smiled at him as he spoke, which seemed to make him sound more confident as he continued the eulogy.

After the service, people gathered in the church's fellowship hall for the reception. The usual awkwardness of such events was heightened by the circumstances. No one really knew how to make small talk when the deceased had been murdered.

I was getting coffee when I noticed Angela approaching Grayson near a memorial photo display. I heard her say, "Grayson, could I talk to you about something? Privately?"

He nodded, and they moved toward a corner of the fellowship hall. I couldn't hear their conversation, but Angela looked agitated. Whatever Angela was telling him seemed to surprise Grayson. His eyebrows raised up, and he pulled out his phone to take notes.

"It was nice of you to come," said a voice behind me.

I turned to find Rebecca there, looking elegant in a black dress and subdued makeup. She was watching Angela and Grayson's conversation with a slight frown.

"I wouldn't have missed it," I said. "David seems like he was a great guy. I wish I'd known him better."

Rebecca nodded. "I keep thinking about the last time I saw him. He seemed really worried about something, but I thought it was just the play. He could be a perfectionist with his work, and I figured that applied to his volunteering, too."

"It was terrible news about Carol, too," I said.

"Oh my gosh, yes. I can't even wrap my head around it. I mean, I was having trouble adjusting to the fact David was gone, now Carol is dead, too? It's just unbelievable. She's been a staple in the art community for decades. I don't know how they're going to survive without her."

I said in an offhand way, "When did you hear about Carol?"

"Well, I was out-of-touch the whole day yesterday. The real estate market in Whitby has picked up lately. Of course, it usually does in the summer months, but it seems even busier than usual. I showed a few houses, spoke to a few clients on the phone, then I headed home to answer emails. Right before I turned in, I received a group email from theater people that Carol had been murdered." She shook her head. "Like I said, it's unbelievable."

"Do you think it has anything to do with David's death at all?" I asked.

Rebecca's brow furrowed. "With David? What could it possibly have to do with David?"

It didn't seem to me that Rebecca was connecting the dots very well. But maybe that wasn't fair. She'd been under a lot of stress lately. Her fiancé had broken up with her, and then had been murdered. She'd mentioned the police considering her a suspect. So maybe she thought that the small-town murders of two people involved in a theater production weren't related.

"Just that they were both part of the Whitby Playhouse group," I said mildly.

Rebecca blinked at this, considering the implications. "Maybe someone was dissatisfied about what was going on with the production. Or maybe David and Carol knew something about somebody involved with *The Spirit of '76*."

"Were there people unhappy with the way things were going at the theater?" I asked.

Rebecca looked rueful. "Well, Carol was. But now it seems pretty unlikely that she murdered David, doesn't it? After all, she's been murdered, herself."

"What was Carol upset about?"

Rebecca said slowly, "Oh, it was really nothing. You might know that Carol taught high school drama for decades."

"She was my teacher, actually."

Rebecca raised an eyebrow. "Did you have acting aspirations?"

"No, but I needed an elective and had heard great things about Carol. She almost made me consider it."

Rebecca said, "I see. As you can probably imagine, being in charge of a classroom for so long meant she was used to being in charge. She was the one who decided on the plays, on the costumes, on who got the roles. When she started in community theater, Carol wasn't in charge anymore."

"But surely she got over that. She'd been retired for a while. It seems sort of petty to let something like that bother her." And I didn't think of my former teacher as a petty person.

Rebecca said, "I don't think Carol was being petty, actually. It was more that she had a different perspective on how to run the show. One that David didn't share. When she tried voicing her opinion, he basically ignored her. I think she was feeling hurt. That was her entire career, and David sort of dismissed her experience."

"That must have been tough for Carol to handle," I said. "And maybe David, too. From what I've heard, he was a caring person. Maybe he started realizing Carol was feeling left out."

"Or maybe not," said Rebecca with a shrug. "I totally agree that David was a caring person. That's why I started dating him to begin with. But he also didn't necessarily pick up on subtext or undertone. He was a person you needed to be direct with. If you hinted that your feelings were hurt, he wasn't going to pick up on it. You'd have had to come out directly and voice your concerns."

I said, "That makes sense. Of course, as you mentioned, it seems unlikely that Carol took out her frustration on David, since she's now been murdered herself."

"Right. Of course, since you were asking if people were upset at David because of theater stuff, there's also Janet McKenzie." She rolled her eyes.

"Did David and Janet have issues?"

Rebecca said, "Oh, sure. Janet wanted *my* role in the play, can you believe it? Martha Washington." Her tone indicated she didn't think that would have made for good casting.

I asked, "And she held David responsible for not getting the part?"

"That's right. I mean, you really can't win when you're a director of a play. But you'd think Janet, of all people, would understand if you don't get a role. She teaches drama at the high school! Anyway, she was definitely displeased about that." Rebecca glanced around. "You can see that she didn't show her face today."

She was right. I hadn't noticed Janet in the sanctuary or at the reception. "Got it. It sounds like there were definitely some folks unhappy with David recently."

Rebecca hesitated, glancing around the room. She looked strained, and I could see the toll from the last week in the shadows under her eyes. "They're not the only ones, either. I probably shouldn't say this, especially not here. But I think David's biggest source of stress was family stuff."

"Meaning Angela?"

Rebecca said, "It's just that Angela's been having a tough time since her divorce. David would worry himself sick over her and her kids." Her voice dropped. "David would come over to my house sometimes looking really upset. When I asked if he was okay, he'd say something about Angela making choices he didn't understand."

"That must have created some tension between them. I mean, if David brought it up with his sister."

"Which he totally did," said Rebecca. "They had arguments over it. David said he'd offered to help with Angela's expenses, but he wanted oversight with her finances if he did. He said Angela had been really offended by his offer. I don't know all the details, but he was definitely worried about it."

Before I could ask anything else, Angela appeared beside us. Her face was tense, but she kept her voice low. After all, we were still at her brother's funeral reception, and people were glancing over in curiosity. In a town like Whitby, not much went unnoticed.

"Rebecca, could I speak with you privately for a moment?"

Rebecca nodded, looking nervous. "Of course."

Angela said, "Excuse us, Ann."

They moved away, and I stepped toward a refreshment table. But I could still hear Angela's voice, tight with emotion.

"I don't think you have a right to be here, Rebecca. Maybe it's time you left."

Rebecca spoke louder than she might have intended. She sounded indignant and on the verge of furious. "What are you talking about? David and I were going to be married."

"*Were* is the operative word there, don't you think? Look, I know you and David were arguing. For all I know, he's dead because of you."

Rebecca gave a disbelieving laugh. "You're kidding me. I would never do something like that. You *know* that, Angela. I loved David. We had our differences with each other, sure, but we cared about each other. And we were reconciling."

Angela cut her off before she could say more. "That's what you say. But David isn't around to contradict you. What I do know is how angry you were that David broke off the engagement. Were you angry enough to murder him? Was it just a split-second decision, or did you plan it?"

Rebecca seemed frozen in place.

Angela's voice grew colder. "David didn't like something you were doing. He didn't approve. And no matter what people might say about David, he had principles. Unlike you."

Tyler appeared at his mother's side, his teenage face set in protective lines. "Everything okay, Mom?"

Angela looked at her son, and I could see her pulling herself together for his sake. "Yes. We were just finishing up."

As Angela walked away with Tyler, her composure intact but fragile, I couldn't help but notice how Rebecca watched them go. Her expression seemed less like guilt and more like fear.

Most of the mourners had filtered out of the fellowship hall by the time Angela approached me again. I was helping stack chairs when she appeared at my side, looking exhausted but composed.

"Ann, I owe you an apology," she said quietly. "I'm sorry I interrupted your conversation with Rebecca like that. I shouldn't have blown up at her, at least not here."

"You don't need to apologize. I know what a tough day this must be for you."

Angela managed a wan smile. "Thanks for understanding. I just couldn't stand the thought of her being at the memorial, acting like she cared about David. Especially after what she did to him."

"You believe Rebecca was involved in David's death?"

She sighed. "I don't know what to think anymore. But I do know David was miserable during the last few weeks of their relationship. Something she did really hurt him, and he wouldn't tell me what it was. He just said he couldn't trust her anymore."

Angela continued, her voice dropping. "The police asked me where I was when Carol Winters died. I mean, seriously? The cops seem to think I'm some kind of crazed killer instead of a mom just trying to cobble her life together. Yesterday afternoon I was showing houses all day. I showed three different properties to two different clients. But they still acted like I was guilty." She shrugged. "They said I could have murdered Carol between clients. Seriously? I'm not exactly a criminal mastermind."

"Ugh, that's awful. I'm so sorry."

"Yeah, it hasn't been easy since David died. I've been feeling guilty because he and I were arguing. Then I've been trying to deal with the kids' grief, which has been tough. And now they think I killed somebody I barely even knew."

I said, "So you and Carol weren't really close."

"Exactly. Like I told the police, why would I murder somebody who was practically a stranger? I mean, I knew who she was. Everybody in Whitby knew who she was. She'd been teaching absolutely forever. But we didn't exactly move in the same circles. Carol was clearly all about theater and art, and I'm just trying to keep my head above water with work and the kids."

"Wait, wasn't Carol helping with David's play?" I asked, trying to sound casual.

"Oh, right. I forgot about that." Angela's response came a beat too late. "I mean, I know she was helping with the production somehow. But David and I weren't really talking much about the play. We were talking about just the usual stuff siblings talk about." She glanced around the nearly empty hall. "I should probably get the kids home. This has been a long day for all of us."

As she walked away, I heard a voice behind me.

"Ann."

I turned to find Burton walking up, looking unusually formal in his dark suit instead of his uniform. He'd been standing near the back of the room during most of the reception, quietly observing everything taking place.

Chapter Fourteen

"Hey, Burton. How are you holding up?" I asked.

His expression softened slightly. "It's been hectic, I'll grant you that. Belle and I had to postpone a little weekend trip we'd planned. It was nothing major, just heading to the beach for a few days with her son before school starts back up again." He gave a rueful smile. "It's not exactly a time to kick back and relax right now, though. Not with two unsolved murders in the space of a week."

"How is Belle doing? And her little guy? I haven't seen them at storytime lately."

"Oh, they're both good. Belle's been a trooper, you know? She gets it that my work has to come first right now. We'll have to come by the library soon, though. Marcus has been asking when we can come hear Luna read again." Then Burton's expression became more serious. "Back on the topic of work, I wanted to ask you if you could provide some insight into your conversations today. I saw you talking to both Rebecca and Angela."

I glanced around the fellowship hall, but it was empty aside from the custodian. "Angela seemed really convinced Rebecca had something to do with David's death. She blew up at her, actually, telling her she shouldn't be here. Angela basically accused Rebecca of killing him, asking if it was planned or a split-second decision."

Burton asked, "What did Rebecca say to that?"

"She completely denied it. Rebecca said she loved David and that they were reconciling. But when Angela kept pressing her about David not approving of something Rebecca was doing, she just seemed to freeze up. She looked more scared than guilty when Angela walked away."

Burton said, "Gotcha. Good to know. What about your earlier conversation with Rebecca? Before you were interrupted by Angela?"

"You didn't miss much today, did you?" I asked wryly.

"Nope," said Burton in a cheerful voice. "That's my job."

"Well, Rebecca mentioned that David and she had some differences, but she really dwelt on the fact that David and Carol had issues with each other. She said Carol was used to being in charge from her teaching days and felt hurt when David dismissed her experience with the theater. Of course, that's not super-helpful, considering the fact Carol was murdered, herself."

Burton asked, "Did Rebecca point to anyone else as being suspicious?"

"Not really. She seemed focused on explaining away the problems David had with Carol, then with defending herself when Angela confronted her." I paused. "Angela also told me she was showing houses all afternoon yesterday when Carol was killed."

"That's true, but she still had the opportunity in-between clients," said Burton. "What was your impression of Angela when she talked about Carol?"

I considered this. "She claimed she didn't really know Carol. I guess they didn't run in the same circles."

Burton nodded. "It doesn't seem so. Of course, it doesn't matter if someone knew Carol well or not—if Carol knew something about David's death, the killer would want to eliminate her."

"And that's what you think happened?"

Burton said, "It might be. But right now, we're not sure."

"You know I don't usually talk about what patrons do at the library, but Carol's dead and this might matter. She was on one of our computers a couple of days ago. She seemed like she was doing some kind of research, although she minimized her screen when I walked up, so I couldn't see what she was doing."

Burton frowned. "Research for a play or something?"

"No, I think it was more regarding David's death." I shook my head, frustrated. "I don't know that for sure, of course. It was more of a gut feeling. Carol didn't say much about what she was doing, but she seemed satisfied, like she'd corroborated something. I could tell you which computer she was using, if that helps."

Burton shook his head. "That's probably not enough info for me to take in one of the library's computers. It would be different if it was Carol's personal device. But there will be all kinds of searches and data from all sorts of patrons on there. But I appreciate you telling me about it. It bolsters the theory that Carol knew something." He glanced at his watch. "I better be heading out. Where's Grayson?"

"He had a source he's been trying to talk to for weeks for another story. The guy was finally free, so Grayson had to talk to him right then."

After Burton walked away, I helped finish stacking chairs in the now-quiet fellowship hall. After finishing, I was getting my purse when I heard familiar voices from the hallway outside the fellowship hall. Following the sound, I found Luna chatting with Stephanie Walsh, one of our regular storytime moms.

"Oh, Ann," Stephanie looked up. "Luna was just telling me about finding poor Carol yesterday. That must have been so awful for both of you."

"It was a shock," I said, accepting the hug Stephanie offered. "How are you holding up, Luna?" Although I'd seen her in the sanctuary, listening to Jeremy's eulogy, I hadn't had the chance to speak with her yet.

Luna gave a smile that was less sparkly than usual. "I'm better today. Staying busy has definitely helped." She turned to Stephanie. "Ann was one of Carol's former students."

"I've heard she was a great one," said Stephanie. "And she was still so involved with drama in Whitby. I was just telling Luna that I saw Carol before she passed. She was at the community center when I dropped Emma off for craft time."

"Was Carol volunteering at the community center, too?" I asked.

"I think she was getting stuff out of the storage room there. The community center is apparently storing overflow items for the Whitby Playhouse. Anyway, she had her phone pressed to her ear and seemed pretty worked up about something." Stephanie lowered her voice, although no one was around us. "I couldn't help overhearing part of it. She was saying something like 'Look, this isn't right. You're not thinking. I care too much about this to have you screw it up.'"

Luna and I exchanged a glance. "Did you hear who she was talking to?" Luna asked.

Stephanie shook her head. "No, but she sounded kind of disappointed. Like she was trying to talk sense into someone who wasn't listening. At the time, I figured it was about a play the theater was going to put on. You know how passionate people can be about something they really care about. But now I'm not so sure."

"You should definitely tell Burton," I said. "Even if it seems minor, it might help."

After we finished helping with cleanup. Luna and I walked out together. The late afternoon heat was oppressive, and the events of the day had left me feeling drained.

"Where's Jeremy?" I asked Luna.

"After the eulogy, he had to head back to work." She paused. "You know, what Stephanie overheard was interesting, right?"

"For sure. It sounded like Carol was confronting someone about something they were doing wrong. I'm wondering if Carol discovered something that got her killed."

Luna said, "That's what I'm thinking, too. I hate it, though. I mean, Carol was probably trying to do the right thing by telling the person to straighten out. But they obviously thought they'd have to shut her up." Luna slumped, looking discouraged. Then she straightened. "Hey, if Carol made that phone call, it should be easy for the cops to find out who she was talking to. Case closed, right?"

"I hope so. But that seems almost too easy, doesn't it? I'm sure the police have Carol's phone. They'll need to know the time and day Carol spoke with Stephanie, of course."

Luna couldn't be deflated, though. "And Stephanie said she'd call Burton. So now we just need to follow up with Burton to make sure she did. If she doesn't, I'll talk to her."

"Coerce her?" I asked, hiding a smile.

"Oh, it wouldn't really be coercion. Just friendly persuasion. I'll be honest with you, Ann, I'm ready for this to be over with. I want to be celebrating my mom's engagement with her but instead these murders are going on. The police have got to get to the bottom of it."

We chatted for a few more minutes before heading our separate ways. It wasn't like Luna to be down like this. But then, David's death had been upsetting for Jeremy, and Carol's death was obviously a big blow to Luna.

When I reached my cottage, I was surprised to see Grayson's car already in the driveway. I found him on the front porch with Fitz, who was sprawled across his lap in the shade.

"Hi there," I said, settling into the wicker chair beside him. "Nice to see you here early. How did your interview go?"

Grayson tickled Fitz under his chin, earning a contented purr. "It was great, actually. I was relieved to finally catch up with that source. I've been chasing him for weeks."

"It's the county budget article, right?"

"That's the one," said Grayson. "But how did things go with you? How was the memorial service? I hated missing it, but this guy was only available today."

"It was very nice. Jeremy did a great job with his eulogy. And I did have the chance to speak with Angela and Rebecca. Although there was some drama, too, at the funeral reception. Angela directly accused Rebecca of murdering David."

"Seriously?" Grayson's eyebrows shot up. "What did Rebecca say to that?"

I filled him in on the confrontation, my conversations with both women, and what Burton had shared with me. Then I mentioned Stephanie's observations about Carol's phone call."

Grayson was quiet for a few moments. "So Carol was trying to talk someone out of doing something wrong. And now she's dead. That couldn't be a coincidence, right?"

I shook my head. "It doesn't seem likely."

We sat in comfortable silence for a minute, Fitz's purring the only sound.

"Grayson," I said quietly, "what if we're not seeing the whole picture? What if there's something bigger going on that we're missing?"

"Like what?"

I said slowly, "I'm not really sure. But Carol was researching something on the library computer. She looked satisfied, like she'd figured out something. Then she's confronting someone on the phone. After that, she's murdered. Maybe we should take a step back and look at what we know from a different angle."

Fitz stretched luxuriously and hopped down from Grayson's lap, padding over to his food bowl with the eternal optimism of cats everywhere.

"I should probably get some rest," I said, suddenly feeling the weight of the day. "Tomorrow's going to be another long one."

Grayson stood and pulled me into a hug. "Try not to worry too much. We'll figure this out." He kissed the top of my head. "And remember, Burton's working the case. He'll get to the bottom of it." He started heading away before turning around. "Are we still on for venue shopping tomorrow? Let me know if it's too much. I did put together a list of places to go, but it's easy to push it off a couple of weeks or more. I know we planned on doing it before all this started."

"Sure, let's go ahead and knock it out. It'll be nice to have a distraction."

After Grayson left, I settled into my chair with a cup of tea and one of the wedding magazines we'd abandoned days ago. But I had a tough time focusing on flower arrangements and venue options.

Fitz reappeared and claimed my lap, purring steadily as I absently stroked his fur. "What do you think, buddy? Are we missing something obvious?"

He opened one green eye and gave me a look that seemed to say that was entirely possible. Then, he promptly fell asleep.

Chapter Fifteen

The next morning, Grayson picked me up bright and early with a thermos of coffee and a smile to do wedding venue research. I was working, but not until the afternoon.

"Where are we starting?" I asked.

"The Riverside Inn. It's about twenty minutes outside Whitby, overlooking the lake. They specialize in small, intimate weddings." Grayson pulled out of my driveway. "After that, there's a winery in the mountains, just a short drive from the inn. If we have time, we can squeeze in this historic mansion that's been converted into an event space."

The Riverside Inn was beautiful. The innkeeper, a cheerful woman named Patricia, showed us around the property with obvious pride. The ceremony site was a wooden deck extending over the water, with the Blue Ridge Mountains as a backdrop.

"We can accommodate up to sixty guests for the ceremony," Patricia explained. "The reception would be in our main dining room, which opens onto the deck for dancing."

"It's gorgeous," I said, watching a family of ducks glide across the water below.

"The photography would be amazing," Grayson added, taking a few pictures with his phone.

Patricia beamed. "We provide all the tables, chairs, and linens. Our chef can customize a menu to your preferences. And, of course, we have partnerships with florists and musicians in the area."

As we toured the reception space, I tried picturing our guests there. It was a beautiful spot. But something didn't feel quite right.

"What do you think?" Grayson asked as we walked back to the car.

"It's beautiful," I said. "And they seem very professional and organized."

"But?"

I struggled to put my finger on it. "It feels like it would be somebody else's wedding, you know? Like we'd be borrowing their vision instead of creating our own."

Grayson nodded thoughtfully. "I know what you mean. Plus, it's pretty expensive. And we'd have to figure out accommodations for any out-of-town guests, like our college friends."

Our second stop was less formal. Mountain View Winery was nestled in the foothills about forty minutes away. The tasting room was housed in a renovated barn with exposed beams and string lights.

"This is more like it," I said as we walked through the vine-covered arbor where ceremonies were held.

The wedding coordinator, John, was enthusiastic and knowledgeable. "We can do everything from casual backyard-style receptions to formal seated dinners."

"Do you host many small weddings?" Grayson asked.

"All sizes, but intimate celebrations are some of my favorites. There's just something special about celebrating with the people closest to you in a spot like this."

I found myself relaxing during the tour. The setting was beautiful without being overwhelming, and I could imagine our friends here.

"The only drawback," John mentioned as we concluded the tour, "is that we're pretty booked up. The earliest availability would be next fall."

"Next fall? We were hoping for something sooner," I said slowly.

"I could put you on a cancellation list, but I wouldn't count on anything opening up before February or March at the earliest."

We told John to put us on the waitlist, but I was already mentally crossing the winery off the venue choices.

The third place was Whitmore House, a Victorian mansion that had been lovingly restored as an event venue. It was stunning, with original hardwood floors, crystal chandeliers, and period furnishings. When you walked inside, it felt like stepping back in time.

"The photography would be incredible here," Grayson said, again looking through the lens of a newspaper editor.

As beautiful as it was, I thought about logistics. Our guests would need to drive nearly an hour to get here. The formal atmosphere, even though it was lovely, didn't quite match our laid-back personalities. And the cost was definitely above and beyond what we'd budgeted.

On the drive back, Grayson and I were both quiet, processing everything we'd seen.

"They were all beautiful," I said finally.

"But none of them really felt like us," Grayson finished.

"Right. The inn was too impersonal, the winery wasn't available until over a year from now, and the mansion was gorgeous, but too formal." I added ruefully, "Maybe we're being too picky."

"Or maybe we haven't found the right place yet." Grayson reached over to squeeze my hand. "There's no rush. We'll find something that feels right."

As we drove back into town, I felt oddly relieved that none of the venues had worked out. Maybe it was the stress of the past week catching up with me, but the thought of making major wedding decisions right now was overwhelming.

I said, "You're right. There's no rush. Let's put venue hunting on hold for a bit. I think I need to focus on getting through this week before I can think clearly about wedding planning. I thought a distraction would be nice, and it was, but maybe I'm not ready to pick a place yet."

Grayson nodded. "That makes perfect sense."

After he left, I gathered my things for my afternoon shift at the library. I ate a quick lunch, collected Fitz from his sunny kitchen spot, and headed out.

After getting some patron research knocked out in the first hour of my shift, I was ready for the relative respite of film club.

Wilson strode into the community room while I was setting up the popcorn machine before film club met. He cleared his throat, and I turned around. "Hey there, Wilson."

"Hi. I wanted to let you know that Mona and I will be attending film club today."

Mona was a regular there, but Wilson was far more intermittent. "Really? That's great."

"Mona loves Timothy's film selections," said Wilson. He paused. "Actually, she also wanted to announce our engagement to the club members." He blushed, and I hid a smile.

"This is the perfect time for that. Great idea."

Wilson paused again, and I waited for him to say what was on his mind. "Mona also wanted to bring some special refreshments that we shopped for this morning. I believe her thought was to make it more of an engagement party. Or a quasi-engagement party and quasi-film club meeting." He stopped with a small sigh. "To be perfectly frank, I'm not entirely sure what she's intending."

I stopped setting up the popcorn machine. "Well, whatever it is, I'm sure it's delicious. How about if we just skip the popcorn altogether today?"

Wilson looked relieved that I was on board. Aside from giving me large and sudden assignments, he did usually have a rather *laissez-faire* attitude toward my work. He wasn't fond of interfering.

I walked out of the community room for a few minutes to answer a couple of library emails. When I came back in, I found Wilson and Mona unpacking what appeared to be enough snacks for a small army.

"We might have gotten carried away at the grocery store," Mona said with a laugh.

Wilson looked slightly embarrassed. "I decided to err on the side of having too much. We wanted to have adequate options for everyone."

"Movie theaters sell concessions, after all," Mona said cheerfully. "We thought we'd go along with the film theme, but have it be a little more celebratory. Because of the engagement, of course."

I peered into one bag and had to hide a smile. They'd indeed gone overboard. There were three different types of specialty popcorn, various candy bars, soft drinks, and what appeared to be ice cream cups.

"This looks incredible," I said. "Everyone's going to love it. You're going to spoil them for future film club meetings."

Luna arrived wearing a vintage movie poster tee-shirt paired with a flowing skirt covered in film reel prints. She spotted Wilson and Mona arranging snacks and grinned. "You two are just adorable together. How's engaged life treating you?"

Wilson colored slightly again. "Quite well, thank you. We're still adjusting to all the attention our engagement has generated."

"Half the town is talking about wedding plans," Luna said with obvious delight.

"We haven't made any plans yet," Wilson said quickly, looking mildly panicked.

Mona patted his arm in a reassuring manner. "We have all the time in the world to figure that out. And we have a new expert to rely on, too!"

Wilson frowned in confusion at his fiancée before following her gaze over to me. Now *I* was the one to feel mildly panicked.

I could envision Wilson assigning me an entirely new and unwanted project, this time involving wedding planning.

Fortunately, before Wilson could think to ask me to help, Timothy arrived carrying what looked like homemade movie posters and a notebook. Owen trailed behind him, looking excited.

"Hey everybody," said Timothy cheerfully. "I can't wait to show you which movie I picked out."

"What is it?" asked Wilson with some trepidation. Wilson enjoyed films, but his tastes were rather narrow.

Timothy held up a DVD case with a flourish. "*Roman Holiday* from 1953. Audrey Hepburn and Gregory Peck."

Several early arrivals murmured approval. George from the typewriter repair shop had just walked in and given a thumbs-up. "Great choice, man. It's got it all: classic romance and gorgeous cinematography."

More people began filtering in and checking out the new-and-improved snack table with interest. To my surprise, Zelda appeared in the doorway, carrying her ever-present bag of sunflower seeds and looking slightly uncertain.

"Owen here convinced me to try something new," muttered Zelda.

"You're going to love it, Miss Zelda," said Owen. "Timothy picks awesome movies."

Zelda surveyed the room with her sharp eyes, taking in the movie posters, the arrangement of chairs, and Mona and Wilson's elaborate snack display. She gave a sniff. "Can't be any worse than the garbage they play on TV these days. I could use something with a little plot development."

A few minutes later, after everyone had gotten snacks and were seated, Timothy moved to the front of the room. "Okay, everybody. Thanks for coming to today's film club meeting. I was thinking, after a rough week for Whitby, that we could all use something special to watch."

He gestured to the movie poster he'd hung up. "So I picked *Roman Holiday*. It's about this really sheltered princess who escapes from her royal duties for twenty-four hours in Rome, where she meets an American reporter. It's all about finding freedom, finding out who you really are, and . . . " he glanced at Wilson and Mona with a small smile, "unexpected love."

Mona clapped her hands together softly. "Oh, how lovely! I haven't seen this in years."

"And a big congratulations to our very own Wilson and Mona on their engagement!" said Timothy. Everyone gave them a round of applause, and George gave a whistle while the two smiled shyly.

As Timothy dimmed the lights and started the movie, a few latecomers slipped in to get some snacks. I sat between Luna and George, with Fitz having mysteriously appeared to claim a spot on my lap.

The opening credits rolled over shots of Rome, and I felt some of the tension from the last week ease up. There was something therapeutic about being surrounded by friends and neighbors, sharing a classic film.

About an hour into the movie, during the famous Moment of Truth scene, Mona leaned over and whispered to Wilson, "Isn't this romantic?"

Wilson, looking far more relaxed than I'd seen him all week, whispered back, "Quite charming indeed."

When the movie ended, everyone applauded again as Timothy turned the lights back on.

"Well," Wilson said, clearing his throat, "that was quite excellent, Timothy. Very thoughtful choice."

"I loved it," Mona said, dabbing her eyes with a tissue. "Though that ending always makes me a bit weepy."

Timothy grinned. "That's what I love about classic movies. They really make you feel things."

Everyone got up, chatting about the film while throwing away their wrappers and other trash.

Zelda was standing by Timothy, thoughtfully crunching a sunflower seed. Owen hovered nearby, clearly eager to hear her early verdict. "So?" he asked in a hopeful voice. "What did you think?"

"That Audrey Hepburn knew how to handle herself, didn't she? Sometimes you got to give up what you want for what's right. It takes guts," said Zelda in her raspy voice.

"So maybe you'll come to the next film club," said Owen, sounding pleased.

"Didn't say that. Depends on what's showing."

Owen said, "But the point is that it's a surprise. That way people get to watch stuff they probably wouldn't choose to watch for themselves."

"Hmph," said Zelda. Broadening her horizons was apparently not something high on her list of things to do. "We'll see, I guess." Then she saw Owen's face fall. "Okay, I'll go. Even old dogs can learn new tricks sometimes. But I hope it's something funny. I feel like seeing something funny. Or a little more action. All that talking and walking around Rome made me antsy."

Timothy heard the last bit and said, "I'll keep that in mind for the next time I pick one, Miss Zelda."

As the group dispersed and the library returned to its afternoon quiet, I helped Wilson and Luna clean up the community room. My phone buzzed with a text from Grayson. *Hope film club went well. Want to grab coffee when you get off?*

Since I only had a half shift, I texted back that I'd meet him at Keep Grounded in an hour.

Chapter Sixteen

It was a quick walk from the library to Keep Grounded. The coffee shop was a cheerful place with brick walls and light streaming through its many windows. Inviting bookshelves lined the walls, and brightly painted wooden chairs and tables were scattered throughout the space. Since Rufus had died and Mabel Cross had taken over, she'd maintained its welcoming atmosphere while adding her own touches.

I ordered a chai tea latte and settled at a table by the window. Grayson was there in a couple of minutes, his face brightening as he saw me. He got his coffee, then came over to join me. "How was film club?" he asked.

I stood to give him a quick hug. "It was good. Zelda was actually there."

"Zelda? At film club?" Grayson raised his eyebrows. "That's progress."

"Apparently, Owen persuaded her to go. Zelda's been full of surprises since she quit smoking." I took a sip of my latte. "Timothy picked *Roman Holiday*."

"Great film."

I nodded. "Oh, and we had enough to eat to feed an army. Wilson and Mona brought the snacks. It was sweet."

"Those two are in the honeymoon phase of their engagement, aren't they?"

I said, "That's right. Before any wedding planning stress starts up."

The bell above the door chimed, and I glanced over to see Pete Brennan entering the coffee shop. He looked around the room, his gaze settling on our table. After a moment's hesitation, he walked over.

"Hey guys. Hope I'm not interrupting anything."

"Not at all," Grayson said politely. "Please, have a seat."

Pete pulled out the empty chair at our table, but perched on the edge as if he wasn't planning on staying long. He looked as if he were searching for what he wanted to say.

Grayson said, "The staff's been working on your spotlight feature for the paper. It'll probably run in about a week."

Pete looked confused for a minute, as if he were lost in his thoughts. Then he nodded, remembering the interview. "Oh, right. Sure, that sounds great, thanks." He shook his head as if to clear it and said, "Sorry if I'm kind of scatterbrained today. I just keep thinking about Carol. It's all so senseless."

Mabel appeared with Grayson's coffee, and Pete quickly ordered a regular coffee to go. "I can't stay long," he explained. "I just wanted to grab something before heading home."

"How are you doing?" I asked.

Pete's hands were restless on the table, drumming a nervous rhythm. "It's been kind of tough, actually. I keep thinking about how dedicated she was to the Whitby Playhouse and how proud she was to be part of it." He sighed. "I guess everybody associated with the theater is a suspect, since theater stuff was used for the murders. The police asked me more questions today. They wanted to know the last time I saw Carol and what we talked about."

"I'm sure those aren't fun conversations," said Grayson.

"It wasn't. But I told them the truth, of course. I saw Carol at the community center the day before she died, helping her pick up some props we'd stored there. She did seem kind of agitated about something, but then Carol could get wound up about stuff."

I considered that. "Yes, I kind of remember Carol as a teacher who *wanted* to be laid-back, but would get worked up in the week before a performance. She'd be running around trying to make sure the set was perfect, that everybody knew their lines, that the lights were working, that kind of thing."

Pete looked at me with interest. "So Carol was your teacher?"

"That's right. She did a great job." I paused. "Could you tell what Carol was upset about?"

"Not really. But Carol looked frustrated, like she was trying to convince someone of something." Mabel returned with his coffee, and Pete took a cautious sip of the steaming beverage. "She was on her phone, and it sounded like a pretty intense conversation. I was wondering if it was about that stuff Rebecca was doing."

Grayson leaned forward slightly. "What stuff Rebecca was doing?"

"You know. All that business with inflating the historical significance of houses she's trying to sell. You'd think every older home in town has Underground Railroad connections or Civil War significance. But I bet there's no documentation." Pete looked serious. "The thing is, Carol would have been the perfect person to catch something like that. She knew a lot about Whitby's history. Her family had been in town for generations."

I exchanged a look with Grayson. Maybe that's what Carol had been researching when I'd seen her in the library.

"The police haven't mentioned anything about Rebecca's business practices to me," Grayson said slowly. "If they had, I'd have inspected the articles she was writing for the paper."

Pete raised his hands. "Look, I don't have any hard evidence or anything. I just know the old Sheldon house sure wasn't around when Rebecca said it was. That much I do know." He paused, then added. "I feel bad even bringing it up, to be honest. Forget I said anything. Rebecca's been through enough with David breaking up with her and then his murder."

"But maybe Carol discovered something that got her killed," I said quietly.

"Exactly. That's what I keep thinking about. Plus, it's not just the historical stuff. I heard Rebecca's been working with some developer from Belton with some big money involved. If Carol had exposed the whole operation, that developer was sure to have pulled out."

"Have you shared this with the police?" I asked.

"I mentioned it when they interviewed me today." Pete looked genuinely troubled. "I just hope it helps them figure out what happened."

We were quiet for a few moments until Grayson said, "I'm sure this has been tough on the whole theater."

"Janet's been pretty shaken up," Pete said. "She'd known Carol for ages. Carol actually taught her when she was in high school, before she went off to college for theater." He stirred his coffee absentmindedly. "I saw Janet at the grocery store yesterday. She looked like she hadn't slept in days."

"That's understandable," I said. "Losing two people from the Whitby Playhouse in one week has to be devastating."

Pete glanced at his watch. "I should probably get going. I've got some paperwork to catch up on." He stood, pulling out his wallet. "Thanks for listening. It helps for me to talk this over with people who knew both of them."

After Pete left, dropping money on the table for his coffee, Grayson and I sat quietly for a few minutes.

"It sounds like we need to talk with Janet again. Maybe she knows something about what happened to Carol," I said.

"Definitely. It sounded like she's been upset by David and Carol's deaths, but maybe she has something else on her mind."

I nodded, but something was nagging at me. I couldn't put my finger on it, but there was a detail somewhere that didn't sit quite right.

"What are you thinking?" asked Grayson.

"I'm not sure." I shook my head. "It's probably nothing. Just my mind trying to make connections that aren't there. I'm not even sure exactly what struck me as odd or whether it was something I heard today or yesterday."

"Maybe your instincts are picking up on something important." Grayson reached across the table to squeeze my hand. "It might come to you later if you don't try to force it."

We finished our coffees and walked out into the warm air. For a moment, Whitby looked peaceful and normal; the kind of small town where the biggest worry should be whether the high school football team would have a good upcoming season.

I woke up the next morning with that nagging feeling still tugging at the back of my mind. Something in one conversation kept bothering me, but I couldn't quite grasp what it was. Fitz seemed to sense my restlessness, staying closer than usual as I made coffee and tried organizing my thoughts.

The phone rang just as I was settling into my favorite chair to read my book.

"Ann?" It was Grayson, and he sounded a lot more energized than I felt. "I just got off the phone with Janet McKenzie. She wants to talk. Apparently, she's got lots on her mind after Carol's death."

"Oh, great. Did she say when we can meet up?"

Grayson said, "This afternoon, if that works for you. She'll be at the community center taking down some of the stuff from the last theater camp session to set up for the next one. Janet said we could come by around two."

After we hung up, I spent the morning trying to put the murders out of my mind, at least temporarily. I pulled some weeds in my front yard before the HOA police, headed by Zelda, gave me a call. Then I played with Fitz with his favorite toy, which sort of looked like a feather duster on the end of a fishing pole.

I leafed through the pages of one of the wedding magazines while I ate a pimento cheese sandwich for lunch. I wondered what Burton knew of the allegations Pete had made against Rebecca. Pete had said he'd told the police, but who knew how much he really revealed to them?

I grabbed my phone and called Burton.

"Ann," he answered on the second ring. "Everything going okay?"

"It's good. But I wanted to follow up on something from yesterday. Grayson and I ran into Pete Brennan at Keep Grounded, and he mentioned Rebecca was involved in some kind of property fraud. At least, I guess it's fraud. She's selling houses and claiming they have more historical significance than they actually have."

Burton said carefully, "Yeah, we've heard a little about that. And Grayson called me yesterday evening. He was worried about it because he didn't want the paper publishing things that weren't true. We're looking into it."

"What kind of trouble could Rebecca be in for something like that?"

Burton was quiet for a moment. "Well, if the allegations are substantiated, it could range from civil fraud charges to criminal fraud, depending on the scope and the dollar amounts involved. Real estate fraud can be a felony if it involves significant sums or crosses state lines, especially if there's interstate commerce involved with out-of-state buyers."

"That sounds a lot more serious than I thought." I'd been thinking that if the buyers didn't want to press charges that Rebecca might just lose her license or something. But this sounded more like jail time.

"It can be serious, for sure. But we're still gathering evidence. It's way too early to say what charges, if any, might be filed." He paused. "Are you thinking Rebecca is connected to the murders?"

"Maybe. Pete thought Carol might have discovered Rebecca's scheme and confronted her about it. He suggested that's what Carol's phone call was about. That's the call I told you about at the memorial service—the one Stephanie Walsh overheard."

Burton said, "We're looking into Carol's last communications, for sure."

I said, "The only problem is, if Rebecca murdered Carol because she was trying to keep her from talking about her fraud, who killed David? Did Rebecca kill him because he broke off their engagement?"

"Ann, I really can't discuss specific suspects or evidence right now. We're pursuing all the leads, though." His tone softened a little. "I know this is hard. But we're making progress."

After Burton hung up, I continued listlessly flipping through the wedding magazines. Fitz picked up on my mood, watching me with growing concern and giving me a pointed meow.

"You're right, Buddy," I said, reaching over to scratch him under his chin. "I'm overthinking this. Maybe Janet will have some answers this afternoon."

Chapter Seventeen

The community center was busy when Grayson and I arrived that afternoon. Janet spotted us as soon as we walked in and hurried over, looking even more frazzled than Pete had described. Her usually artistic attire was rumpled, and there were dark circles under her eyes that suggested she hadn't been sleeping well.

"You're covering David and Carol's murder in the paper, right?" asked Janet right off the bat.

Janet looked as if there was something she wanted to unload. Grayson wouldn't be printing any rumors or allegations in the paper, not without a lot of verification. But we definitely wanted to hear what was on her mind.

"That's right," said Grayson. "Just trying to get the perspectives of some of the theater community."

Janet nodded, then paused. "There's a small office that nobody's using right now. Let's go in there and talk."

We followed her into a small space off the main room that was cluttered with recreation supplies, board games, and craft supplies. Janet closed the door and plopped into a battered-looking desk chair. She pointed vaguely to some folding chairs propped up against the wall, which Grayson pulled out for us.

Janet sighed. "I apologize in advance if I get emotional. It's just hard to believe that David and Carol are both gone. They were totally dedicated to theater here." She was quiet for a few moments. "I keep thinking about the last conversations I had with both of them. With David, I was still annoyed about the Martha Washington thing. You know, that he wouldn't cast me. Then, with Carol, looking back, I realize I was being so petty."

"What do you mean?" Grayson asked gently.

"Carol came to see me last week, and it sounded to me like she was being critical of my summer theater program. She was the kind of person who took everything in; she didn't miss a thing. I got defensive and said some things I shouldn't have." Janet's hands twisted in her lap. "Of course, now I realize she was probably just trying to be helpful and offer advice, but I was just too proud to see it."

Janet gave a shaky sigh before continuing. "I guess my relationship with Carol was a little complicated. Maybe I never stopped feeling like her student. But I wanted to be respected by her. She never gave a lot of compliments to other adults, although she totally did for her students."

I said, "Could it be that Carol was feeling a little bit envious that you were leading the next generation of theater kids in Whitby? Maybe she was sad that her teaching career was over?"

Janet glanced at me. "I never thought of it that way. You're right, that could be it. She might have just felt sad that she wasn't the one in charge anymore. I should have thought about that."

I said, "It's hard if you feel you're being second-guessed."

Janet nodded again. "Right. Sorry, I took us on a detour because I've been feeling sorry for myself. Carol had wanted to talk to me about something else, not just how I was running the summer camp. She was worried about the theater finances and wanted to bounce some thoughts off somebody. But not someone currently working with the Whitby Playhouse. I guess I should have been pleased that she wanted my opinion, but I was still too caught up worrying about how she thought I was conducting the drama camp."

Grayson said, "Weren't the theater's finances in good shape? It always seems to get excellent support from the community. There are plenty of sponsors, and the shows always sell out."

"It didn't sound like Carol thought the finances were in good shape at all. She was talking about the bookkeeping being off or inflated costs for productions—stuff like that." Janet rubbed her forehead like it hurt. "I wish I'd been paying more attention to her. I hate that it was my last conversation with her and half my mind was focused on getting back to the kids."

I said, "So Carol thought there were irregularities with the bookkeeping?"

"That's what I gathered," said Janet with a quick shrug. "Again, I wish I'd been listening closer."

"Did you tell the police about this?"

Janet shook her head. "I honestly hadn't remembered what she wanted to talk about. I know that sounds crazy, but I was so ridiculously focused on what she said about the way I was handling the summer camps. Whether I had appropriate insurance for the summer program, if the material I was choosing was right for the age groups, if I was being careful enough with safety in ensuring the campers weren't handling dangerous stage equipment." She looked down. "I only just remembered what Carol was saying about the finances. Obviously, I was barely listening to her." Janet rubbed her face. "I didn't remember until I spoke with you, Grayson. Then it finally occurred to me."

"You should tell Burton about this," I said quietly.

"Oh, I will. Maybe it's something important to the case. Maybe someone didn't want her asking questions, right? I know Pete is the bookkeeper for the playhouse. But anyone could have taken money from there. I mean, anyone *involved* in the theater. It's not like someone could have walked off the street and done it. But the box office proceeds were often just kind of sitting out in the ticket office, you know? Someone from the inside could have made a habit of lifting some of it."

Grayson leaned forward slightly in his folding chair. "Janet, you mentioned feeling bad about your last conversation with David and Carol. What happened with David? Besides the casting decision, I mean."

Janet's face crumpled slightly. "Yeah, it was really petty of me. David had come by the community center a couple of weeks before he died. He was checking on props we were storing here for the Whitby Playhouse, and I was setting up for the summer camp. He made some comment about how organized everything looked, and I thought he was being sarcastic."

"Was he?" I asked gently. Janet looked so distressed, so very cognizant of how she'd spoken with David. There was self-disgust on her face.

"Looking back, he probably wasn't being sarcastic at all. David wasn't really a sarcastic person. But I was still so hurt about not being cast as Martha Washington that I took everything he said, every expression of his, the wrong way." Her mouth twisted. "I told him that just because I teach high school doesn't mean I don't know how to run a professional program. I was really snippy about it."

Grayson said, "That's not so terrible to say. Your feelings were hurt about not getting the part. You were lashing out."

"It gets worse," Janet continued. "David tried to apologize. He said he hadn't meant anything by his comment about my being organized. That he was really impressed by what I was doing with the drama camp. But I just couldn't let it go. I kept saying that the established community theater crowd didn't give new people a fair chance." She gave a short laugh. "In retrospect, that doesn't even make any sense. David was one of the 'new people,' after all. He'd only lived in Whitby a few years."

I could see tears forming in Janet's eyes. "David just stood there and took my rant. Finally he said something like 'I hope you know I never meant to hurt your feelings, Janet. I think you're a talented teacher and director.' But I was too worked up to really hear him."

"What did you say?" I asked quietly.

"I told him if he really thought that, he should have cast me as Martha Washington instead of his girlfriend." Janet's voice was barely above a whisper. "I knew immediately I'd gone too far. David's expression just kind of shut down. He said, 'I see' in this tight voice. Then he walked away."

I got up to give Janet a quick hug. She held me tight before releasing me. I settled back in my chair. "You couldn't have known what was going to happen."

"But it did happen," said Janet miserably. "I didn't go to his memorial service because I was so embarrassed about how I'd treated him. I kept thinking about going, but then I'd remember that awful conversation we had. I couldn't bring myself to face Angela or Rebecca. I was worried he'd told them what I'd said."

"I'm sure they would have appreciated your being there," I said. "They know people have arguments." But I thought about Angela's reaction to Rebecca being at the service.

Janet shook her head. "Maybe. But I felt like I'd look like a hypocrite if I went. I kept thinking that if I really cared about David, I shouldn't have been so horrible to him the last time we spoke. Now I'll never get to apologize to him."

We sat in silence for a moment. Then Janet glanced at her watch. "I should probably get back to cleaning up here. I want to have everything ready for the next camp session."

We said goodbye to Janet and walked out into the late afternoon heat. Grayson was quiet until we reached his car.

"Janet's really beating herself up about that last conversation," he said.

"That's human nature, isn't it? I'm sure most of us have wished we could have had a better last conversation with a friend or family member."

We were both quiet, thinking about that, as Grayson drove me to run a couple of errands since we were already out. By the time we got back to my cottage, it was nearly six o'clock. Fitz met us at the door with his usual chirping meow, immediately winding around Grayson's legs as if he hadn't seen him in weeks rather than hours.

"I should call Burton," I said, pulling out my phone. "What Janet said could be important. And I'm not sure how soon she's planning on telling the police about it."

Grayson settled into one of my gingham chairs with Fitz claiming his lap. "Good idea."

"I'll put it on speaker so you can hear, too."

I dialed Burton's number and put the phone on speaker when he answered.

"Ann, what's up?"

"Hi Burton. I've got Grayson here with me on speaker. We just came back from talking with Janet McKenzie at the community center. She wanted to tell us more about her last conversation with Carol."

"I'm all ears."

We filled Burton in on what Janet had said about the bookkeeping being off and inflated costs for theater productions. That Carol suspected there were some irregularities.

"Hmm, okay," Burton said. "That fits with some information we've been checking on. And I'll give you an update on our end, too. We've been able to trace Carol's last phone call. It was to Rebecca Thorne."

Grayson's eyebrows shot up, and I leaned closer to the phone. "You're thinking it might be about the exaggerated listings Rebecca was creating?"

"We're thinking that might be the case. Carol was obviously paying a lot of attention to everything and everybody around her. That may have resulted in her death. We're planning on interviewing Rebecca again tomorrow about that conversation. And I know I've mentioned this before, but the two of you need to be careful. Anybody connected to this case could potentially be dangerous. Stay alert."

After Burton hung up, I settled into the chair next to Grayson. Fitz looked back and forth between us, as if trying to determine whose lap offered better accommodations.

"So Carol's last call was to Rebecca," I said. "That doesn't look good for her."

"Though we still don't know what they talked about. Maybe Carol was calling to talk about something related to the theater."

I said, "But the play was over and done with. Rebecca wasn't exactly a regular at the Whitby Playhouse, from what I've been able to see. When I checked her social media, *The Spirit of '76* was the only play she'd mentioned. She probably got involved in it because of David, when they were still engaged."

"Good point. Maybe Burton will find out what they talked about."

We spent a quiet evening together, trying not to dwell too much on the murders. Grayson helped me make supper, and we talked about lighter topics like the wedding plans, the cottage expansion, and what Fitz's reaction to the sunroom would be. Maybe the pleasant mundaneness of our time together helped me sleep. When I woke up in the morning, I felt blissfully refreshed.

Chapter Eighteen

I arrived at the library just after noon the next day to start my late shift. Fitz had been so relaxed in a sunbeam in my kitchen that I left him in what seemed like a pleasant dream instead of bringing him to the library.

Luna was at the circulation desk, wearing a tie-dyed sundress and looking energetic when I walked in.

"How are things going?" I asked her.

"Better. Much better, actually." Her eyes flashed with determination. "Jeremy and I talked last night and decided it's time to get angry."

"Angry."

Luna nodded. "We're mad that someone thinks they can just kill people in our town and get away with it. David and Carol are gone because some coward couldn't face the consequences of whatever they were doing wrong." Luna's voice grew fierce. "Jeremy's been asking around at work to see if anyone knew what David had on his mind before he died. We're not just going to sit around and wait for the police to figure this out."

I thought about what Burton had said about the danger involved in probing around. Luna must have read my mind because she quickly said, "Oh, we're being careful. But we're also not going to let whoever did this think they've won." She straightened her shoulders. "Jeremy did find out some interesting information from some of David's other coworkers."

"What kind of information?"

"Apparently, David had been asking a lot of questions about financial auditing lately. Apparently, he had some coworkers wondering if *David* was having money problems. But now it sounds like maybe it had something to do with the theater."

I quietly filled Luna in on my talk with Janet the day before. Luna gave a low whistle. "So somebody was swiping money from the Whitby Playhouse. I wonder if David figured out who the thief was."

Before I could respond, Wilson emerged from his office looking harried. "Ann, there you are," he said, completely ignoring Luna as inconsequential regarding whatever his problem was. "We have a situation with the copy machine again. Someone tried to copy a three-dimensional object."

I simply couldn't comprehend what happened to completely sane patrons when they were in proximity to the copier. It seemed like some sort of madness overtook them. "What sort of three-dimensional object?"

"A pinecone. Covered, naturally, in glitter." Wilson looked pained. "And the patron put glittery paper in the paper tray. The repair technician is on his way, but he said this is the third call from us this month. He's threatening to charge us some sort of surcharge for 'creative misuse of equipment.'"

Eventually, I calmed Wilson down. I also dissuaded the repairman from assessing that surcharge. That felt like a full shift right there, but the afternoon was a blur of patron research needs, tech questions, and general cacophony.

Around four o'clock, Zelda settled at a library table with a stack of what appeared to be printed pages from the internet. "I'm not taking any chances with my personal security," she told me grimly.

I was clearly meant to walk over and chat, which I did. It was always important to stay on Zelda's good side. "What's all that?" I asked, gesturing to the stack of papers.

"Home security research," said Zelda. "Motion sensors, security cameras, and those doorbell things that let you see who's there when you're not home. Two murders in the space of a week means it's time to take precautions."

"That sounds very thorough," I said.

"Some of the security systems even call the police automatically if someone breaks in," said Zelda with satisfaction. "And think of all the times I'm not at home. Half the time, I'm working the reception desk at the garage. Or hanging out here." Zelda's gaze swept across the library rather critically, as if questioning her life choices.

"Actually, you *have* been spending a good deal of time at the library lately," I said, the fact just occurring to me. "Have they cut down on your hours at the auto repair place?"

She sniffed. "They told me I had too many hours, and they couldn't afford to pay me overtime. They said I needed a vacation. Ridiculous. So I'm having to take a break for a couple of weeks. And they told me that I couldn't work overtime when I go back."

"It all sounds perfectly reasonable," I said.

Zelda apparently disagreed.

The rest of my shift passed quietly. Around seven o'clock, my phone buzzed with a text from Grayson. He said that he'd left a message for Rebecca to explain whether the newspaper had printed fraudulent claims about recent houses. She'd apparently texted him back in a panic, saying that she wanted to meet with him in person and talk. He'd suggested tomorrow, but she wanted to speak with him tonight. He told her he was wrapping up tomorrow's paper at nine tonight and asked if I wanted to come.

I told him I was closing up the library, but I could be there at 9:15.

I walked the few blocks to the *Whitby Times* office, enjoying the relative coolness of the night air. The small downtown was quiet, with most businesses closed and only a few streetlights illuminating my way.

The newspaper office was familiar territory for me. The narrow building was squeezed between a boutique and a long-closed hardware shop, its front windows giving a warm and welcome glow in the darkness.

I pushed open the front door, setting off the door chime as I walked in. The newsroom was a cramped but efficient space with several desks arranged around the room. Grayson's office was a glassed-in spot in the back and was its usual organized chaos of papers, manila folders, and coffee cups.

Rebecca was sitting in a chair next to Grayson's desk, clutching a tissue and looking like she'd been crying. Even in distress, she maintained her professional appearance, but there was something fragile about her that I hadn't seen before. Grayson seemed relieved to see me.

"Thanks for coming," Grayson said in a low voice, standing to give me a quick hug. His expression was tense, and I could see frustration in his eyes.

Rebecca gave me a tight smile. But she looked relieved to see me, too, maybe because I would provide a buffer between her and Grayson. If she'd knowingly printed false statements in the paper, Grayson was definitely not happy.

"I'm sorry," Rebecca said quietly. "I know I shouldn't have done it. Printing something made-up in the paper is wrong. I know that."

Grayson waved his hands in agitation. "It's also wrong to sell houses under false pretenses. You were selling houses that weren't actually historical at all."

Rebecca pressed her lips together, blinking quickly. "No, I wasn't. But I didn't kill anybody. You've got to believe me. The cops think I did, but they're wrong."

I didn't want Rebecca to know that Burton had told me Rebecca was Carol's last phone call. So I asked, "Why do the police think you did it?"

Rebecca sighed. "Because Carol called me shortly before she died. But that doesn't mean anything."

"Did you pick up the call?" I asked.

Rebecca nodded. "I was showing a house to clients, but when I saw it was her, I stepped outside to take the call. I thought it was maybe something to do with the theater."

"Instead, I'm guessing it was about your fraud. She obviously knew about it," said Grayson. I could hear the edge in his voice. He cared a lot about the veracity of what he printed in the *Whitby Times*.

"Carol was furious with me. She'd been researching the properties I'd written about in my historical columns for the newspaper." Rebecca's voice grew quieter. "She knew I'd been less than truthful about their historical significance."

"Less than truthful? You mean you lied about it," said Grayson.

Rebecca said, "Look, I'd just been embellishing the historical importance of some properties I discussed in the paper. And some of the ones I was listing, sure. After she'd found out the truth, Carol called to say she'd found documentation that I'd fabricated most of it."

"You fabricated historical information for articles in my newspaper." Grayson's voice was flat now, carefully controlled. But I could see how angry he was.

Rebecca gave a quick nod of her head again. "I never meant for it to go this far. It started really small. I'd just mention that a house was 'historic' without being specific. But then I started getting clients who were particularly looking for properties with historical significance. I'm talking about wealthy buyers from out of state who were willing to pay premium prices."

I said, "And you created the historical significance to meet the demand."

"Exactly. It worked so well that I kept doing it. I was making so much more money than I'd ever made before. But Carol figured it out. I'd never seen her act that way before."

"Act how?" asked Grayson.

"Mad. She was totally furious. She said I was damaging Whitby's real historical legacy because I was mixing truth with lies."

The mention of lies made Grayson agitated again. "You put the whole reputation of the newspaper at stake, Rebecca. People rely on us to be credible, and I've been publishing false information. I'm going to have to go through and print tons of retractions for these articles."

"I know, and I'm so sorry," Rebecca said, fresh tears starting. "I was going to tell you, I promise. I was trying to figure out how to come clean about everything."

"When?" Grayson asked sharply. "When were you planning to tell me you'd been lying in print for months?"

"I don't know. Soon. David had already figured out what I was doing. He was so disappointed in me. It's the whole reason he broke our engagement. He said he couldn't marry somebody who'd lie for money."

I asked, "Was David going to expose you?"

"No. Absolutely not. He was angry, but he wasn't going to go to the cops or tell Grayson or anything." Rebecca stopped short. "Wait. Are you thinking I killed David because I was scared he was going to tell everybody I exaggerated some stuff in print?" Her voice was disbelieving.

Grayson said, "Why wouldn't we think that? It was more than exaggeration, Rebecca. It was fraud. As far as I know, you might have done anything to cover up illegal activity and avoid jail time."

Rebecca said quietly, "That's what the cops think, too. It's what everybody will believe when this comes out."

I asked, "What did Carol say when she confronted you?"

Rebecca sighed. "I mean, that was a tough conversation, too. Not quite as bad as having an engagement broken, but pretty bad. I begged Carol not to expose me. I told her about my contract with the developer in Belton and how much money was involved. I said it would ruin me if the truth came out. I asked her for some time. I even offered her some money to stay quiet."

"And what did Carol say?" I asked.

"She was offended I even tried to buy her off. She said lying about history was serious, and that I needed to face the consequences of what I'd done. Carol told me she was going to call Grayson the next day to discuss pausing the column until I could verify all my historical claims." Rebecca's face clouded at the memory.

Grayson asked, "Carol was going to call me?"

"That's what she said. She wanted to make sure the newspaper wasn't complicit in spreading false information." Rebecca looked up at us with her red-rimmed eyes. "That's the last time I spoke with her."

We sat in silence for a moment. Then I asked, "And you were showing houses when Carol was murdered."

"That's right. And the police verified that. But they still say I could have slipped away in between showings." Rebecca shook her head. "It's such a mess. I mean, I understand why the police suspect me. But I didn't kill Carol, even though I know how it looks. I was already planning on coming clean because I knew what I was doing was wrong. Losing David was a wake-up call for me. I realized how far I'd strayed from the person I wanted to be."

"How much of this have you told the police?" I asked.

Rebecca gave a short laugh. "Not all of it. I wanted to talk to Grayson and explain myself before I ended up getting arrested. And I wanted to tell you in person, not over the phone or in a text or email. I'm sorry, Grayson. I promise, I really am." She paused. "There's one other thing I haven't told the cops. Actually, I haven't told anybody. Since it was during my conversation with Carol, I didn't exactly want to share it."

"What is it?" I asked.

"Right at the end of my conversation with Carol, she said something like 'you're not the only one who needs to do the right thing.'" Rebecca looked at both of us. "It sounds like she was planning on confronting someone else. Maybe the person she confronted decided to shut her up permanently."

Grayson asked, "Carol didn't say anything else about who that person was?"

"No," Rebecca said, shaking her head. "Carol didn't give me any clues about that. But she sounded determined, like she'd made up her mind about something important."

Grayson looked solemnly at Rebecca. "You've got to fill Burton in on everything you told us. Now that I know the full picture, it's not something I can just sit on."

"No, you're right. And maybe it'll help him find out who killed Carol. Can you two stay here while I talk to him?" Rebecca looked nervous again. "I'll be less flustered with someone else here."

Grayson nodded. "Sure, that's fine with me."

I said, "I'm afraid I'm going to have to get back home; I'm pretty wiped. But I'm sure it's going to go smoothly. I'll get Grayson to update me later."

"Of course," said Rebecca. "This might take a while, and it sounds like you've had a long day."

I stood up. "I'm sure Burton can sort this all out."

"Thank you both," said Rebecca, looking genuinely grateful. "I know I've made a mess of things, but I really am sorry."

"Need me to walk you back to your car?" asked Grayson, looking concerned.

"I'll be careful. It's just a minute back to the library."

The short drive home from the library parking lot gave me time to decompress a little. I had further decompression when Fitz met me at the door with a chipper meow. He wound around my ankles, then sat back and studied my face with those intelligent green eyes of his.

"It's been quite a day," I said as I scratched him behind his ears. He gave me what seemed like a reproachful look. "Sorry I didn't take you to the library this afternoon, buddy. You were just so happy in your sunbeam when it was time to go."

I changed into my pajamas and made myself a cup of chamomile tea. I settled into the gingham chair with the cottage expansion plans Grayson and I had been looking at. Fitz clambered onto my lap, purring loudly.

The plans were a welcome distraction from the murders and investigations. I traced the proposed lines for the new sunroom with my finger, imagining how it would look with morning streaming through floor-to-ceiling windows. Fitz would love a sunny spot for his afternoon naps. The kitchen floor was all well and good, but the sunroom would be even better.

"What do you think about this layout?" I asked Fitz. "It looks like we can add the space without changing the cottage's character."

He opened one eye, gave the plans a cursory look, then apparently decided they met with his approval. He stretched, resettled himself more comfortably, then resumed his purring.

I was feeling drowsy when my phone rang. It was Grayson.

"How did it go with the police?" I asked.

"Better than I expected. Burton listened to everything Rebecca had to say. He seemed to believe her story. She said that the property fraud sort of snowballed, but that she had nothing to do with Carol's death." Then Grayson paused. "At least, Burton seemed like he believed her. Who knows? Maybe that's just me being hopeful. I tend to think Rebecca isn't lying. I'm furious with her, but I don't think she's a killer."

I said, "But Burton's still considering her a suspect?"

"Probably. He seemed more interested in the property fraud as a separate issue than in Rebecca as a murderer. He's going to coordinate with state authorities about potential charges related to the real estate violations. He was interested in what Rebecca said about Carol planning on confronting someone else."

I said, "I'm guessing he didn't have any theories about who that might be."

"Well, not that he shared with us. But he's going to re-interview some of the other people involved with the Whitby Playhouse to see if anyone knows what else Carol might have discovered."

After we hung up, I turned in. But I found myself tossing and turning with too much on my mind. Fitz carefully retreated to the far end of the bed for a quieter spot.

Chapter Nineteen

I was enjoying a peaceful breakfast on my front porch the next morning when I spotted Zelda marching up my front walk. She was carrying what appeared to be several official-looking pamphlets and had the determined expression of someone with important business to conduct.

"Good morning, Zelda," I called out, setting down my coffee cup. "Everything going okay?"

"As well as it can be without cigarettes," she grated. She settled herself in the wicker chair next to mine without waiting for an invitation.

"Want some coffee?" I asked, gesturing to my cup.

Zelda looked at her watch. "I've got to work at the garage today, but I think I have time for a cup."

"Cream and sugar?"

"I take my coffee black," said Zelda in a rather offended tone, as if I was suggesting some sort of flibbertigibbet nonsense.

I returned to the porch in a few moments. In the interim, Zelda had spread out several of the glossy brochures on the small table between us. "I got my new alarm system installed. Motion detectors, door and window contacts, cameras, the works. And one of those video doorbells. I'm leaving these pamphlets so you can take a look. I'm thinking you need some security yourself. You're still living alone, after all."

"Thanks, Zelda," I said. "That's thoughtful of you. It all sounds very comprehensive. Are you feeling more secure now?"

"Better. At least when it comes to that stuff. But now I have something else on my mind." Zelda fixed me with a stern look. "I heard through the grapevine that you and Grayson might be planning an addition to your cottage. You do know you have to get the HOA architectural committee to approve anything in advance, don't you?"

I sighed. Of course, Zelda would know about our expansion plans within days of us discussing them. "Yes, I'm aware of the HOA requirements. We're still in the very early planning stages. Really, we're just bouncing ideas around."

"Well, make sure you follow the proper procedures. The architectural committee meets the third Thursday of every month." Zelda pulled out a small notebook and flipped through several pages. "I've documented all the requirements you'll need to meet."

"Thanks," I said, although I wasn't entirely sure I meant it. Then I said, perhaps a little snippily. "Not much gets past you, does it?"

Zelda gave a moody sigh. "Sure it does. That murderer, for instance. Killing people in Whitby." Zelda's expression indicated she took it as a personal affront. "Although a lot doesn't get past me. I believe I saw you and Grayson heading to the community center the other day." She gave me a curious look. Maybe more of a nosy look. "Are you planning to have your wedding reception there?"

I certainly wasn't going to tell Zelda anything I didn't want broadcast throughout the entire town. "Actually, Grayson and I were there to interview Janet McKenzie for a piece Grayson is writing on how the community is coping with David and Carol's deaths."

"Ah, Janet McKenzie. I know who she is." Zelda gave a satisfied nod, as if visiting Janet had been her first guess. "She's a busy woman, isn't she? I've seen her recently."

"Oh?"

"That's right. She was hanging around the theater building right around the time that poor Carol woman was murdered," said Zelda.

My coffee cup paused halfway to my lips. "Janet? Are you sure it was her?"

"Of course I'm sure," said Zelda crossly. "I was driving back from the bank. I like to have lots of small bills and those ATMs don't spit out in fives and tens." She sounded like she might go on a tangent about ATMs, but reined herself in admirably. "Anyway, I saw her there. I figured she was there to help clean up after that patriotic play or something."

"Janet wasn't in *The Spirit of '76*," I said.

"Sure she was," said Zelda. "She does that play stuff."

"Janet auditioned for a part, but didn't get it. She's been working on giving summer drama camps to children instead."

Zelda's eyes narrowed suspiciously. "Well then, what was she doing there the day Carol was killed?"

"What time did you see her?" I asked.

"It must have been ten o'clock. Maybe a smidge after." Zelda took a noisy slurp of her coffee, then leaned forward conspiratorially. "Maybe Janet did it. I always said that woman had too much nervous energy. All that artistic temperament bottled inside."

When Grayson and I had talked to Janet, she'd said she was at the community center with her summer camp when Carol was murdered.

"Zelda, are you sure it was Janet you saw?" I pressed her again.

"Of course I'm sure! I might be getting older, but my eyesight's still twenty-twenty. There's nothing wrong with my brain, either. Plus, Janet's got that distinctive way of walking. It's all quick and jerky like she's always running late." Zelda studied my face with her sharp eyes. "You look kind of tired, Ann. Aren't you sleeping?"

I hesitated. Part of me thought Zelda should call Burton and fill him in. But I'd noticed she had a tendency to jump to conclusions and sometimes embellish details. Before involving Burton, I wanted to talk to Janet myself and give her a chance to explain.

"I'm not sleeping great, no," I admitted.

"Hmph. Probably because of the killer running around. Take a look at my alarm system brochures. And I'll keep an eye out for Janet. She bears watching. Too much coincidence for my liking. If she wanders through the neighborhood, she'll have a nasty surprise in store."

After Zelda left, I sat on my porch for a long time, thinking. If Janet had been at the Whitby Playhouse, why hadn't she mentioned it when we talked to her?

I glanced at my watch. I didn't have to be at the library until after lunch, which gave me some time. I didn't want to jump to conclusions like Zelda tended to do, but I also couldn't ignore what she told me.

I spent the morning running errands and thinking things through. I had some wedding magazines Grayson and I had already perused that Mona had asked to borrow. The library had some wedding magazines, but they were perpetually checked out, so these were some I'd bought. I figured I could drop those off at the library for Wilson to bring to her.

I was downtown picking up a prescription when I spotted Wilson and Mona emerging from the historic church. Wilson was clutching a thick folder and looking stressed out.

"Hey, you two," I called out, jogging over.

Mona's face lit up when she saw me. "Perfect timing, Ann. I'm dragging Wilson around to venues for the church and the reception. I was dying for him to show off the comparison matrix he came up with."

Wilson looked slightly embarrassed. "I've simply organized our options logically. Each venue has been rated on capacity, acoustics, parking availability, historical significance, and cost per guest."

I hid a smile. "Wow, that's . . . thorough."

"Would you like to join us for our next stop?" Mona asked. "We're looking at the community center, and I could use a second opinion."

"Sure, I've got time before work." I also thought it would be interesting to see Wilson's systematic approach to wedding planning in action. I had the feeling it would be a good deal different than the venue visits Grayson and I had made.

At the community center, the director showed us the main hall. Wilson immediately began questioning her about logistics while Mona wandered around the space, touching tables and checking out what would be the serving area.

"What's the per-hour rate?" Wilson asked, making detailed notes. "Are there additional fees for set-up? What about restrictions on outside vendors?"

The director's phone rang, and she excused herself briefly to take the call.

"It's a bit institutional, don't you think?" Mona asked me quietly.

"It's economical," Wilson replied. He frowned at the space, though, as if trying unsuccessfully to picture a wedding reception there.

"It's also where the elementary school holds their summer lunch program," Mona pointed out gently. "I can still smell fish sticks."

Wilson said slowly, "I thought cost-effectiveness was our primary consideration."

"Along with ambiance," Mona reminded him. "Remember? You said you wanted our wedding to be memorable."

"This would certainly be memorable," Wilson muttered, eyeing a suspicious stain on the carpet.

"Ann, do you think you can join us for the next stop?" asked Mona.

"I think I have time for one more," I said. It was far more relaxing to venue shop when it was someone else's wedding instead of my own.

The next stop was the botanical gardens on the edge of town. As we walked through the entrance, I smiled as I saw Wilson's formal posture starting to relax. It was a nice afternoon with the temperatures warm but not too hot, with a gentle breeze rustling through the trees.

"Oh my," Mona breathed, stopping near a fountain surrounded by white flowers. "Wilson, this is beautiful."

For the first time all afternoon, Wilson set down his folder on a nearby bench. "It is rather pleasant," he admitted.

The gardens event coordinator showed us several locations. As we walked toward the pavilion overlooking the pond, I watched Mona slip her hand into Wilson's.

"Wouldn't it be lovely here? With all the flowers and the sound of the fountain?"

Wilson looked around, his folder forgotten. "It's quite romantic," he said, his voice softer than usual.

I knew Wilson would eventually want his practical considerations addressed. I asked the coordinator, "Are there weather backup plans or catering facilities?"

The man assured us there were covered areas and preferred caterers familiar with the space.

Wilson nodded, but his heart didn't seem to be in the paperwork anymore. He was watching Mona, who had wandered over to smell some lavender.

"The gardens will require substantially more coordination," Wilson said to me quietly.

"But?" I prompted.

"But Mona looks happier than I've seen her all day." Wilson adjusted his tie, always a sign he was making an important decision. "Perhaps the additional complexity is justified."

As we walked back to the parking area, after a short detour when Wilson remembered to get his folder from the bench, Mona was practically glowing. "Wilson the gardens would be perfect. I know it's more complicated than the church reception hall, though."

"Mona," Wilson said gently, "if you want the botanical gardens, we shall have the botanical gardens."

Mona stopped and kissed his cheek. "Have I mentioned lately that I love you?"

Wilson turned pink. "Perhaps once or twice."

"Well, I do. Even when you're making matrices for our wedding venues."

"*Especially* then?" Wilson asked hopefully.

"Yes, especially then."

As we reached the cars, Wilson was already pulling out his phone. "I should start speaking with those preferred caterers."

"Wilson," Mona laughed, "we just got engaged. The wedding isn't until next spring."

"Proper planning prevents poor performance," Wilson replied seriously. "I want everything to be perfect for you."

"It will be perfect because we'll be getting married. Everything else is just details."

Wilson looked at her for a long moment, then carefully put his phone in his pocket. "You're absolutely right. Though I still intend to create a comprehensive planning timeline."

"I wouldn't expect anything less," Mona said fondly.

By the time I arrived at the library around noon with the wedding magazines I'd grabbed from the cottage, I'd decided to call Janet and ask her to come in during my shift. I could frame it as wanting to follow up on something from our last conversation, which was true enough. If she had an innocent explanation for being at the playhouse (and if Zelda was actually correct that it was Janet in the first place), then I'd hear her out.

The library was busier than it had been recently. Luna was at the circulation desk wearing a colorful sundress that somehow managed to incorporate every color of the rainbow.

"Can't stay away, can you?" she asked, grinning at me. "You're early for your shift."

"I brought some wedding magazines for your mom," I said, holding up the stack. "I think she was wanting to leaf through for ideas."

"Oh, let's stow those out of sight. If you leave them lying around, a patron will go running off with them. Those things are popular here. Maybe I'd better let Wilson take them to Mom. Jeremy and I are supposed to be going out to supper tonight. And I know she'll want to see the magazines right away."

I said, "She sounded really excited."

"Totally. She's been driving Wilson crazy with all her planning ideas. Well, you know. I hear you went on their venue-viewing expedition."

"They were kind of cute today about it all, actually. It was a shame I didn't have the magazines in the car when I joined them." I peered over at Wilson's office. "Looks like Wilson's back."

"Yep, wrestling with the quarterly budget reports. He'll be grateful for the interruption."

I knocked on Wilson's office door and entered when he called out. He was indeed surrounded by spreadsheets and looked slightly frazzled.

I held up the magazines. "I brought these by for Mona."

Wilson's expression softened immediately at the mention of Mona. "That's very thoughtful of you. Thanks." He paused, looking slightly embarrassed. "I confess I'm somewhat overwhelmed at the prospect of planning for a wedding. There seem to be a lot more decisions involved than I was aware of. Mona keeps showing me pictures of flowers online and asking my opinion on color schemes. And you saw how complicated the venue visiting was."

"If it helps, I don't think there are any *wrong* decisions," I said. "It's supposed to be fun. Although it can end up being stressful."

"Is it stressful for you at all?" asked Wilson.

"I wouldn't say it's stressful, not right now at least. I'm just looking forward to the big day, and the planning helps me feel closer to it."

"Indeed," said Wilson. He carefully moved the magazines to a clear spot on his desk. "I'll be sure to take these home with me this evening. Mona really wants to start making concrete plans."

"Well, just remember to call if you need any advice on planning. Grayson and I are learning as we go, too."

Chapter Twenty

I settled back at the reference desk and tried to focus on my work, but my mind kept drifting to Janet. Finally, I pulled out my phone and sent her a text, asking if she could stop by the library to follow up on our conversation. I told her I'd be at work until nine p.m.

Her response came back quickly. *Of course! I can be there around 7:30 if that works.*

I told her it did, then stared at my phone, second-guessing myself. Should I be calling Burton instead of asking Janet directly? But if Zelda had been mistaken, I didn't want to cause unnecessary drama.

The rest of the afternoon passed slowly. A few patrons came and went. Wilson emerged from his office looking harried. He left around five-thirty, but I was speaking with a patron and couldn't see if he'd remembered the magazines. Luna finished her shift at six.

"You sure you're okay closing by yourself?" Luna asked as she gathered her backpack that doubled as a purse.

"I probably close up the library a couple of times a week," I said gently.

"Yeah, I know. It's just with the murders, it makes it a little different."

"I'll be fine," I said. "There was an email that went out from the town saying Burton had increased patrols downtown. Anyway, there'll probably be a few patrons here until we close. I'm always having to wake someone up who's nodded off over a book."

Luna nodded and headed out for her dinner with Jeremy. As the library grew quieter, I found myself checking the time more frequently. I was ready to talk to Janet and listen to her side of things.

At exactly 7:30, Janet walked through the library doors. She looked tired but smiled when she saw me at the reference desk.

"Hey there," she said in a friendly voice. "Is Grayson getting you to follow up on interviews for him now? I didn't know that was one of the duties of a fiancée."

I took a deep breath, trying to sound casual. "Actually, it had more to do with Carol's death than the story Grayson's working on. I remember you said you were at the community center, but someone thought they saw you at the Whitby Playhouse around that time."

Janet's face froze. For just a moment, an emotion I couldn't quite identify flickered across her features.

"Oh," she said, her voice carefully controlled. "Who told you that?"

"Does it matter? What's more important is whether it's true or not." But I could tell from her expression that Zelda was right. Janet, for whatever reason, had been there. Which meant I'd need to follow up with Burton to tell him.

Janet looked around the library, noting that we were alone except for an elderly patron browsing in the history section. She moved closer to my desk and lowered her voice.

"I knew how it would look," she said under her breath. "I was already a suspect because of my issues with David. If the cops knew I was at the theater when Carol died, it was going to make things even worse."

"But why were you there?"

Janet said fiercely, "Because I'm an idiot, that's why. I'd been feeling so guilty about how I'd treated David. I thought I should go and apologize to Carol for how I'd spoken with her."

"So you went to the playhouse to make things right?"

Janet nodded. "I'd been feeling awful about how defensive I'd been when she came to see me. I knew she was probably just trying to help. I was giving myself a hard time because, after all, I've been so guilty about how I'd spoken to David. I felt like I wasn't learning any lessons from that. So I decided to speak with Carol in person."

She paused, looking around her again. But the same elderly patron was still in the distance, flipping through a book. "I knew Carol was usually at the playhouse in the mornings, organizing stuff over there. So I drove over. But when I walked inside, I found her in the storage room. She was already dead." Janet gave a shudder, remembering.

I said slowly, "And you didn't call the police."

"I didn't. I know how it sounds. I thought about calling them, but then I realized how it was going to look. They were going to get totally the wrong impression. Like I said, I knew I was already a suspect in David's death, and it would look even worse if I called in about Carol. So I just left. I left her there."

I said, "Janet, you have to tell Burton about this."

"But I wasn't even there when she was killed. I didn't see or hear anything helpful. If I call the police, they're going to waste their time investigating *me* when they could be looking for whoever the actual killer was."

I said, "You still need to call Burton. Even if you have an alibi, you found the body and didn't report it. Maybe you can help narrow down the time of death."

"I know, I know. I should have called the cops immediately." Janet looked miserable. "But I was scared. After David's death, people were already looking sideways at me because of our argument. I didn't want to give anyone more reasons to suspect me."

"Burton's fair. Just explain what happened."

Janet sighed. "It's going to look even worse now that I waited so long to say anything."

"It'll be a lot worse if they find out themselves that you were there and you never reported it."

Janet was nodding. "Okay. I'll call Burton first thing tomorrow. But I'm not going to do it tonight. I'm so exhausted right now that I can barely think straight. I don't want to try to explain myself when my brain is so muddled."

"Go get a good night's sleep," I said.

Janet headed out. I tried to get back to working on the library newsletter again, although my brain was finding it hard to focus. A few minutes later, the library doors opened again, and I looked up, halfway expecting to see Janet there again. Instead, it was Pete Brennan. He did occasionally come into the library from time-to-time, usually after work to chill out with periodicals. This time he came up to the reference desk first to speak with me.

"Hey, Ann," he said. "Thought I'd slide by here before you closed." He glanced around the library, noting the man still perusing the history section. "Seems like a quiet night here. Does that mean you close up early?"

"No, we stay open until nine, no matter what. You never know when someone will slide by to pick up a book they have on hold or to ask a question about their homework."

Pete nodded absently. "Got it." He paused. "I was thinking back to the conversation we had about Carol. The more I think about it, the more I feel like Janet could be the one the police should be after." He gave me an apologetic look. "Sorry for bothering you with this. It's just that we were talking about people who might have had a motive to do something to David and Carol, and I just remembered something about Janet. I figured while it was on my mind, I'd come over."

"No, that's fine. I can't get the murders out of my mind, either. Why are you thinking Janet might be involved?"

"The insurance office isn't far from the Whitby Playhouse, you know. I just remembered seeing Janet near where Carol was murdered." He grimaced. "I know I should talk to Burton about it, but I wanted to pass it by someone else first to make sure I'm not too far off-base. I know Janet doesn't exactly seem like a serial killer or anything. She works for the school, for crying out loud."

Of course, I already knew Janet was near the theater, although I didn't want to tell Pete that. The elderly man in the history section slipped out the door without checking anything out. "Was there any other reason you thought Janet could have done something like that?"

"She's seemed really stressed out lately. I mean, she's over at the Whitby Playhouse pretty regularly because she'll do a play sometimes. I've seen her there plenty of times before. Anyway, she was mad at David about not getting a part in his play, which I'd forgotten to mention. Maybe Carol knew Janet had killed David and had to be murdered to silence her?" He shook his head. "Is this even making sense? Do you think I should let Burton know about this?"

I said, "It sounds like something he should be aware of, for sure."

"It's just that I started thinking it had to be someone with access to the theater supplies, right? Since David and Carol were murdered with theater supplies. That takes inside knowledge."

A chill ran down my spine. Something clicked in my mind. It was that nagging detail that had been bothering me since I'd heard it. Pete mentioned at the coffee shop that both victims were killed with theater equipment, but that information had never been made public. The police had been careful to keep those details out of the newspaper. How did Pete know about it?

I tried to keep my expression neutral, but my heart was starting to race. "If you have any questions about Janet, you should definitely call the police. How about if I call Burton now?"

Pete must have picked up on my change in demeanor because his expression shifted. The helpful, concerned citizen mask slipped away, and I saw something harder beneath.

"You figured it out, didn't you?" he said quietly. "I thought you might have."

Chapter Twenty-One

I tried to keep my voice steady. "Pete, if you're having problems, there are people who can help."

"Help?" Pete let out a bitter laugh. "Ann, I've been taking money from the Whitby Playhouse for over a year. Just small stuff to help me keep my business afloat. But then my kids' college tuition payments came due and the insurance business got worse." He ran his hands through his hair. "It was supposed to be temporary. I was going to pay everything back."

I slowly reached for my phone, but Pete noticed the movement.

"I wouldn't do that if I were you," he said, his voice taking on a harder edge. "You don't really understand the full picture."

"I think the full picture is pretty clear, don't you? David figured out you were stealing funds from the Whitby Playhouse. He confronted you about it on July Fourth. You didn't want him to tell anyone, so you murdered him with a rubber mallet from the theater to keep him quiet. That's what happened," I said, managing to keep my voice steady.

"David was going to destroy my family," said Pete in a leaden tone. "I was going to lose everything. Brennan Insurance had been around for three generations. I didn't want the business to die on my watch. Plus, I was going to have to pull my kids out of college. I know my wife would have left me when she found out. Everything I'd been working for over the years would be gone. I was in an impossible position."

I knew I had to keep Pete talking if I had any chance of getting away. If he got distracted enough, maybe I could tap in 911 on my phone and alert someone that way. "Come on, Pete. You had choices. Lots of kids take out college loans; I was one of them. And maybe your wife wouldn't have left. You don't know what she'd have done. David and Carol would still be alive if you'd just been honest." I inched my hand toward my phone.

Pete said hoarsely, "Carol was worse than David. At least David told me he'd give me time to think about reporting myself before he did it. Carol told me she had documentation proving what I'd been doing."

"The financial records were at the theater?"

Pete said, "Of course. That's where they'd always been kept. If I'd taken the accounting home with me, it really would have made everybody suspicious."

He paused, fuming. I put my hand casually over my phone on the desk. Then he continued, "Nobody wanted anything to do with the accounts. They were just grateful somebody was handling them and that it wasn't them. But then Carol started poking around."

"So Carol had proof? What kind of documentation?" I carefully slid my fingers on the side of my phone to turn the phone on.

"Yeah, bank records, stuff like that." He brooded about the inconvenience of Carol for a few moments. The library felt unnaturally quiet. Even the usual hum of the air conditioning seemed muted. I was acutely aware of how isolated we were, and how dark it was getting outside as it got closer to nine o'clock.

"You went to the playhouse to talk to Carol. She'd called you before she confronted you?"

Pete said, "No, she confronted me when I was already at the theater. I guess she saw my car there and went inside. She'd been reorganizing the supplies, which is how she started getting into the bank statements and other stuff. I asked her to keep quiet." He gave a short laugh. "I *begged* her to keep quiet. You don't think I wanted to murder *Carol*, do you? Of course I didn't. I told her about my family and the fact my grandfather started the insurance business."

"She didn't listen," I said quietly. I needed to look at my screen to get the keypad pulled up to make the call. That meant I'd have to pull my phone off the desk and into my lap, out of sight.

"Carol said it was too late for explanations. She'd already made up her mind to call Burton right then and there." His hands clenched into fists. "She wouldn't listen to reason."

I gently pulled the hand holding my phone toward me. But Pete spotted the motion. His eyes narrowed. "What have you got there, Ann?"

My heart stopped, and I felt a cold, clammy sweat.

Then the library doors swished open. Pete and I both froze.

It was Wilson. "Ann? I forgot those magazines for Mona." He stopped, sizing up the situation between Pete and me. "Mr. Brennan," he said slowly. "Is everything okay?"

I could see in his keen eyes he'd picked up on the tension. He'd always been observant, even if he wasn't the best in social situations.

I said urgently, "Wilson, be careful. Pete's the one who murdered David and Carol." I called 911 and put my phone on speaker.

Pete looked like his mind was reeling, like he was trying to work out what to do. The 911 operator came on, and I quickly filled her in.

"I need to go," Pete said abruptly, starting for the door.

Wilson, despite his usual formal demeanor, moved with surprising agility to position himself between Pete and the exit. "Mr. Brennan, I really must insist you stay until the authorities arrive."

Pete stopped, looking trapped. His shoulders sagged as the reality of the situation hit him.

"The police are on their way" the 911 operator's voice came through my phone. "Stay on the line and remain calm."

Fitz, sensing the tension in the room, had positioned himself near the circulation desk and was sitting very still, ears slightly back as his green eyes stayed fixed on Pete.

"Pete," I said gently, "running will only make things worse. If you cooperate with Burton, it'll be much easier."

"Cooperate?" Pete let out a bitter laugh. "Two people are dead because of me. There's no cooperating my way out of this."

He slumped into one of the nearby library chairs, putting his head in his hands. "What am I going to tell my kids?"

Wilson, ever the librarian, even in crisis, pulled out his phone. "Perhaps I should contact Grayson?"

I nodded gratefully. "Yes, please call Grayson. He'll want to know." My call to 911 was still ongoing.

The next few minutes felt like hours. Pete sat motionless, occasionally muttering about his family and the insurance agency. Wilson tried to look ominous, but was mostly just out of his element. Fitz had given up being comforting and was now sitting alertly by the front door as a lookout.

"How long have you been taking money from the theater?" I asked Pete, partly to keep him talking and partly because I wanted to better understand. Although there was no way to understand the violent death of two innocent people.

"It's been about eighteen months," Pete said without looking up. "I started out small with just a hundred here, a couple of hundred there. I really did mean to pay it back as soon as business started picking up at the insurance agency." His voice cracked a little. "It never did pick up. My son needed money for his dorm deposit, and my daughter's tuition was due. Nothing ever went in my favor."

Things had gone a lot less in David and Carol's favor.

Wilson's phone buzzed. "Grayson is on his way," he reported.

Just then, we heard sirens approaching. Fitz's ears perked up, and he padded over to peer out of the door into the darkness.

"The police are nearly here," I said to the 911 operator, who ended the call.

Pete looked up with red-rimmed eyes. "I never planned for any of this to happen. When David confronted me before the parade, I just snapped. I was in a total panic. David had been using the mallet to secure the bunting anchors before setting it down to adjust the fabric. I grabbed it without thinking." He couldn't finish.

I said, "That was risky. Half the town was at the parade."

"I wasn't thinking about the *risk*," said Pete impatiently. "Not the risk of somebody seeing me, anyway. I was thinking about the risk of David telling the police what I'd done. He was going to put me in a lot more danger."

"And Carol?" Wilson asked quietly.

"She had it all figured out," said Pete with a shrug. "She'd been going through old records and comparing bank statements. I guess she'd gotten suspicious about the amount that was in the bank and decided to do some digging. She told me at the theater that she had proof and was going to speak with Burton immediately. I begged her to give me time, but she said it was too late for that."

The sirens were louder. Through the large library windows, I could see the flashing lights approaching.

"She just wouldn't listen," said Pete, sounding exhausted. "She said stealing from the Whitby Playhouse was a betrayal of everybody who'd ever volunteered there. But she didn't understand what I was going through." He shook his head and repeated, "She wouldn't listen."

Burton rushed through the library doors, followed by a deputy and a state police officer. He took in the scene quickly, seeing Pete slumped in defeat, Wilson standing guard, me still by the reference desk, and Fitz now calmly observing from his perch on the windowsill.

"Everybody okay?" Burton asked immediately.

"We're fine. Wilson got here just in time."

Burton nodded, then turned to Pete. "Mr. Brennan, I need you to stand up slowly and put your hands where I can see them."

Pete complied without resistance. "I might as well make a confession. But there were extenuating circumstances."

"We'll discuss everything down at the station," Burton said, signaling to the deputy. "Right now, you're under arrest for the murders of David Hollister and Carol Winters."

Chapter Twenty-Two

As Burton read Pete his rights, Grayson came rushing through the door. He crossed the room in three quick strides and pulled me into a tight hug. "Are you okay?"

"I'm fine," I said, leaning into his embrace. "Wilson saved the day."

Wilson looked a bit embarrassed by the praise. "I simply forgot Mona's magazines. It was serendipity really."

Grayson looked around the scene, and I followed his gaze. Burton's deputy and the state police officer were escorting Pete to the door. Wilson, who seemed to suddenly have nervous energy, had started organizing books in a display. And Fitz was now grooming himself as if nothing out of the ordinary had happened whatsoever.

After the police left with Pete, the three of us stood in the suddenly quiet library. The normal evening sounds like the hum of the computers and the ticking of the wall clock sounded unnaturally loud after all the drama.

"Well," Wilson said, adjusting his tie, "this has certainly been an eventful evening. Perhaps we should close the building?"

"That sounds like an excellent idea," I said.

Grayson coaxed Fitz into his carrier as I gathered my things behind the reference desk. Wilson said dryly, "Perhaps we should consider adding 'emergency procedures for apprehending criminals' to our staff training manual."

Despite everything, I found myself laughing. "We handled it just fine with our current skill-set."

We headed to the parking lot, Grayson carrying Fitz in his carrier. Wilson locked up behind us, and we stood for a moment in the parking lot under the streetlights.

Grayson said, "Ann, I can drive you home and drop you back off at the library tomorrow to get your car. It's been a rough night for you."

"I'm okay," I said. "Just wiped out."

"Are you sure?" he asked, frowning.

"Positive. Go write your story for work. I'm all good."

Wilson cleared his throat. "If I might say so, Ann, you showed remarkable composure and quick thinking tonight. I'm proud to have you as a colleague."

This was high praise indeed, coming from Wilson. "Thank you. And thanks for coming back for those magazines and handling the situation so well. If you hadn't come back, it might have ended completely differently."

"Indeed," said Wilson, adjusting his tie. "Mona's wedding planning fixation has some merit after all."

We said our goodnights, and I drove home through the quiet streets.

A few days later, Whitby was slowly returning to normal. I spotted Burton with his girlfriend Belle and Belle's son Marcus near the town square when I was out running errands. It was the first time I'd seen Burton so completely relaxed since the murders began.

Marcus was carrying what appeared to be a plaster cast of some kind, gesticulating excitedly as he explained something to Burton. Burton was crouched down to Marcus's eye level, examining the object with the same serious attention he brought to police evidence.

"That's excellent detail work," I heard Burton say as I approached. "You can see individual toe prints clearly."

Marcus said, "I know you think it's a raccoon, but I still think it could be a bear."

Belle noticed me first. "Ann! How are you doing? I heard all about your standoff in the library with Pete Brennan. That must have been terrifying."

"It was definitely more excitement than I wanted. But Wilson arrived at exactly the right moment, and Burton wasn't far behind."

Marcus tugged on my pant leg. "Did you know that Burton's going to get me a real magnifying glass? Like detectives use?"

"That sounds very useful for your nature investigations," I said.

Burton looked fondly at Marcus, ruffling his hair. "He's a natural observer. He needs to have the right tools for examining evidence."

"Evidence like animal tracks and leaf patterns," Belle added with a laugh. "Not crime scenes."

"Mom, let's go to the park. I want to look for tracks there."

Belle looked over at Burton, who said, "I'll catch up with you in a minute."

We watched as Belle and Marcus headed toward the park. Burton said, "Are you really holding up okay?"

"I'm much better now that it's over. How are you?"

"Relieved," said Burton. "Pete confessed everything once we had him in the interview room. He just broke down completely. He kept saying he never meant to hurt anybody."

"Is Pete still being held in town?"

Burton shook his head. "No, the state police transferred him to county holding. The DA's office will handle the prosecution from here." He sighed. "You know, as many years as I've done police work, it never ceases to amaze me how desperation can make people act out. I knew Pete in passing, of course, but the people who I've talked to who've known him their whole lives tell me they'd never have guessed he could do something like this."

"That's got to be the hardest part about cases like this," I said. "When it's somebody you know, who seems like a good neighbor."

Burton nodded grimly. "The theater group is trying to figure out how to move forward, which is probably going to be an emotional process as well as a financial one. They've had a huge loss, if you think about it. Two active members murdered and one arrested. Then there's the money side of things. They're going to have to do a complete audit and figure out how much was taken." He glanced toward the park where Belle and Marcus were looking at the ground. "But that's not my problem anymore, thankfully."

"It's got to feel good to close a case like this."

"It does. Sometimes you work cases where you really never know if you got the right person. This isn't one of those."

Marcus's voice carried across the square. "Burton! Come see what I found!"

Burton smiled. "That's my cue. It's either going to be a track or a rock. Marcus found some interesting rocks for his collection earlier today."

"Don't let me keep you from rock or track examination duties," I said with a grin.

Later, I was sitting on my front porch with Grayson, watching the sunset and finally feeling like I could breathe again. Fitz sprawled across both our laps, purring contentedly.

"Have you heard anything about how Angela and the others are doing?" I asked, taking a sip of my iced tea.

"Better than you might expect," Grayson said. "I've been following up for the newspaper coverage and checking in with everyone involved. Jeremy's been keeping me updated, too. He and Angela have stayed in touch since David's memorial service."

"How about Rebecca?" I asked. "I was wondering if she was facing charges for the fraud."

"Her real estate license is suspended pending investigation, but she's not facing any criminal charges. It turns out the property fraud was mostly civil violations. Obviously, she's not working for the paper any longer," said Grayson. "And Janet's doing well, too. The community center asked her to take over coordinating all their arts programming."

I said, "I have the feeling she might be more involved with the Whitby Playhouse, too, considering it's lost both David and Carol. How about Angela?"

"Angela is probably doing the best of all of them. David left her a substantial inheritance, so she can pay off her debts and not worry about money for a while. She mentioned getting counseling for her kids to help them process everything that happened."

"I'm glad to hear that."

We sat in comfortable silence for a moment, listening to the evening sounds of the neighborhood. Somewhere down the street, someone was mowing their lawn. A dog barked playfully in the distance.

"You know," I said, "a week ago I was worried about wedding planning and cottage renovations. Now those problems seem pretty manageable in comparison."

Grayson chuckled. "Speaking of which, we should probably get back to that planning. We've got a wedding to organize and a house to expand."

I said, "I liked the idea of the spot for morning coffee in the sunroom with Fitz supervising. We'd be able to see the sunrise from there."

"Sounds perfect to me," said Grayson.

Fitz opened one green eye as if to approve of the plan, then settled back into contented purring.

"Have you thought any more about where you want to have the wedding and reception?" Grayson asked. "We've looked at pretty much all the options. Well, between our venue trip and the one you took with Wilson and Mona."

I said, "Actually, I have an idea about that."

"Oh?"

"What if we had it here? In the garden behind the cottage? It would be small and intimate, and we could celebrate our wedding and the start of our life together."

Grayson's face lit up. "That's perfect. We could set up chairs under the oak tree and maybe string up some lights."

I nodded. "And maybe Wilson could walk me down the aisle. I'm feeling very fond of Wilson, especially considering he saved my life."

Just then, I spotted Zelda walking up the street with Owen, both of them carrying what appeared to be takeout dinner bags. She waved when she saw us.

"Still no cigarettes," she called out cheerfully. "Owen and I are celebrating with Chinese food while his mom runs some errands."

"Congratulations, Zelda!" Grayson called back.

Owen beamed proudly at her, then said, "Miss Zelda's alarm system caught a raccoon trying to get into her garbage last night."

"Those motion sensors and the alarm system are good," she said with satisfaction. "Though I still think a good umbrella is the best defense in most situations."

After they walked away, Grayson and I looked at each other and burst out laughing.

"I love this town," I said.

"Even with all its murderers, property fraud, and overzealous HOA members?"

"Especially because of them. They're *our* murderers, fraudsters, and HOA members."

Grayson leaned over to kiss me tenderly, avoiding disturbing Fitz. "So garden wedding it is?"

"Garden wedding it is."

Fitz stretched luxuriously across our laps and gave a meow that sounded remarkably like approval. After all, he'd be gaining a sunroom out of the whole arrangement. From his perspective, everything was working out perfectly.

And from my perspective, he was absolutely right.

About the Author

Bestselling cozy mystery author Elizabeth Spann Craig is a library-loving, avid mystery reader. A pet-owning Southerner, her four series are full of cats, corgis, and cheese grits. The mother of two, she lives with her husband, a fun-loving corgi, and a couple of cute cats.

Sign up for Elizabeth's free newsletter to stay updated on releases:

https://bit.ly/2xZUXqO

This and That

I love hearing from my readers. You can find me on Facebook as Elizabeth Spann Craig Author, on Twitter as elizabethscraig, on my website at elizabethspanncraig.com, and by email at elizabethspanncraig@gmail.com.

Thanks so much for reading my book…I appreciate it. If you enjoyed the story, would you please leave a short review on the site where you purchased it? Just a few words would be great. Not only do I feel encouraged reading them, but they also help other readers discover my books. Thank you!

Did you know my books are available in print and ebook formats? Most of the Myrtle Clover series is available in audio and some of the Southern Quilting mysteries are. Find the audiobooks here: https://elizabethspanncraig.com/audio/

Please follow me on BookBub for my reading recommendations and release notifications.

I'd also like to thank some folks who helped me put this book together. Thanks to my cover designer, Karri Klawiter, for her awesome covers. Thanks to my editor, Judy Beatty for her help. Thanks to beta readers Amanda Arrieta, Rebecca Wahr, Cassie Kelley, and Dan Harris for all of their helpful suggestions and careful reading. Thanks to my ARC readers for helping to spread the word. Thanks, as always, to my family and readers.

Other Works by Elizabeth

Myrtle Clover Series in Order (be sure to look for the Myrtle series in audio, ebook, and print):

Pretty is as Pretty Dies

Progressive Dinner Deadly

A Dyeing Shame

A Body in the Backyard

Death at a Drop-In

A Body at Book Club

Death Pays a Visit

A Body at Bunco

Murder on Opening Night

Cruising for Murder

Cooking is Murder

A Body in the Trunk

Cleaning is Murder

Edit to Death

Hushed Up

A Body in the Attic

Murder on the Ballot

Death of a Suitor

A Dash of Murder
Death at a Diner
A Myrtle Clover Christmas
Murder at a Yard Sale
Doom and Bloom
A Toast to Murder

Mystery Loves Company
A Murder Down Memory Lane
Murder Sees All (late 2025)

The Village Library Mysteries in Order:
Checked Out
Overdue
Borrowed Time
Hush-Hush
Where There's a Will
Frictional Characters
Spine Tingling
A Novel Idea
End of Story
Booked Up
Out of Circulation
Shelf Life
Dead Silence
The Sunset Ridge Mysteries in Order
The Type-A Guide to Solving Murder
The Type-A Guide to Dinner Parties
The Type-A Guide to Natural Disasters (2025)
Southern Quilting Mysteries in Order:

Quilt or Innocence
Knot What it Seams
Quilt Trip
Shear Trouble
Tying the Knot
Patch of Trouble
Fall to Pieces
Rest in Pieces
On Pins and Needles
Fit to be Tied
Embroidering the Truth
Knot a Clue
Quilt-Ridden
Needled to Death
A Notion to Murder
Crosspatch
Behind the Seams
Quilt Complex
A Southern Quilting Cozy Christmas

MEMPHIS BARBEQUE MYSTERIES in Order (Written as Riley Adams):

Delicious and Suspicious
Finger Lickin' Dead
Hickory Smoked Homicide
Rubbed Out

And a standalone "cozy zombie" novel: Race to Refuge, written as Liz Craig